No Sex Please, I'm Menopausal!

By

Stevie Turner

No Sex Please, I'm Menopausal!

Copyright Stevie Turner 2014
All Rights Reserved

No part of this book may be reproduced in any written, electronic, recording, or photocopied form without written permission of the author. The exception would be in the case of brief quotations embodied in the critical articles and reviews and pages where permission is specifically granted by the author Stevie Turner.

Although place names are real, all names of characters and the characters themselves are fictitious. Any similarity to any persons living or deceased is purely coincidental.

Thanks to LLPix Designs for the front cover, and Obsessed by Books Designs for the back cover. Also thanks to Becky Stephens for giving me instructions on how to edit my manuscript, and last but not least to Caleb's Book Formatting Service.

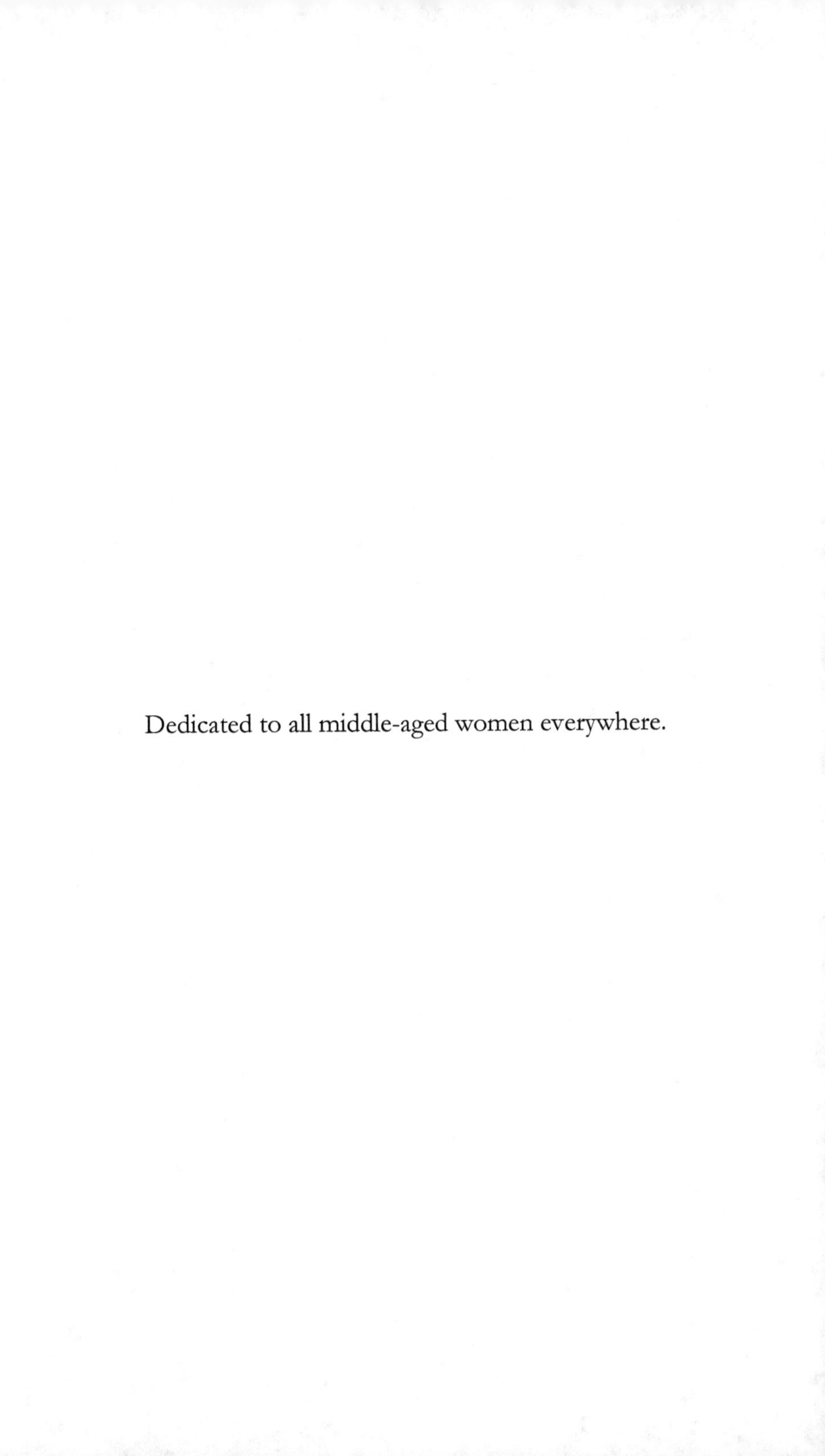

Dedicated to all middle-aged women everywhere.

Synopsis

After going through the menopause Lyn finds that she no longer wants sex. This is unfortunate, as her husband Neil still does. When he discards her after 35 years of marriage like an old worn out shoe, Lyn moves to Cornwall to start a new life. However, new friends are hard to find, and she feels lonely. On the spur of the moment she decides to join an online dating site, 'MatchULike', just for companionship. Amongst the peculiar people she meets is Peter; shy, and conscious that his 'gentleman's' operation has rendered him an unattractive prospect in the marriage stakes. Lyn makes a friend of Peter, but when Neil gets to hear about the friendship he realises too late that there is more to a relationship than just sex, and he suddenly starts to appear back on the scene and wants to turn her life upside down all over again!

Table of Contents

CHAPTER 1

"SORRY, BUT IT'S still the same as when I told you the last time and the time before that. It's too painful, and I haven't got a vagina anymore!" Lyn Fuller sighed as she removed her husband's wandering hand. "Can't you just accept it?"

From a clear vantage point between his wife's legs, Neil Fuller let out an expletive as he risked a quick second glance.

"Yes you have, I can see one!" His finger pointed directly towards the object of the dispute.

"It's for exit purposes only."

"Shit."

"No, that's the other end."

"Well, can't you stick something up there to help?" He took another glimpse; his erection deflating rapidly as he spoke.

"Wild yam is supposed to do the trick if you can't take HRT."

"Eh? You've got to stick a yam up there?" Neil looked quizzically at the size of the introitus on display, mentally comparing it to the dimensions of the root vegetable.

"Wild yam *cream*, dickhead." She rolled her eyes.

"What good would that do?" He exhaled forcefully.

"I've no idea, but what else would you suggest?"

"How the fuck do I know? Ask the Quack for some bombers or something?"

"You mean pessaries?"

"Yeah."

Lyn felt the mattress give a little creak of protestation as her husband flopped down onto the pillow.

"What am I supposed to do then? Tie a knot in it?"

"You know I don't want to take HRT. Pessaries are also full of oestrogen, and you chucked away the KY, so if the wild yam cream's no good then we're stuffed."

"Or not, as the case may be." Neil had a sudden enlightening thought. "Marlon Brando used butter in 'Last Tango in Paris.'"

"Well I wouldn't fancy spreading it on my bread after you've dipped your willy in it, and Maria Schneider shot him at the end anyway, so it didn't do him any good in the long run." Lyn closed her eyes and wished his obsession with sex would go away. "And no, you're not sticking it in there either. Yeah, I saw that film too."

She opened up one eye to watch as her husband turned over on his side, lifted himself up on one elbow, and reached over to turn off the lamp.

"We're only in our fifties. Does that mean twenty or thirty years plus with no sex then?"

"There are other ways; you know that. It's all about getting used to the new normal and accepting it." Lyn shuffled over towards him and cuddled up to his warm back.

"I don't want to get used to it."

"Well, I'm afraid you're going to have to. My body is fifty five years old. I'm not the nineteen year old I was when we first met."

"You can say that again. You were as randy as a sack full of rabbits back then." A small smile played on Neil's lips in the darkness, as he enjoyed a brief wave of nostalgia.

"But now thanks to Mother Nature I have no oestrogen. No oestrogen equals no hormone fluctuations, no randy feelings, and unfortunately no vagina. I can't even have an orgasm; not that I'd want one now anyway. However, there is one good thing about it."

"You don't say." Neil sniffed dismissively and pulled the duvet up around his ears.

Lyn snaked an arm around his waist and whispered into his ear: "I don't get any periods."

"Woop-de-doo-dah."

"I thought you'd be pleased all the PMT has gone now."

"I'm so pleased that I'm going to jump out of bed in a minute and do a little dance around the room."

"Don't think you've been spared either. You're in the dangerous age for a man-o-pause. Everyone knows that. Men your age start to think they're twenty again. They buy big motorbikes, get tattoos and earrings, and start chasing younger women."

"Yeah? I can't wait. When can I start? At least it sounds better than your hot flushes."

"Hot flushes are not just a woman's prerogative. I read about it; if a man has a low testosterone level he'll get hot flushes as well. It's just nature's way of trying to bring the levels back up."

"Low testosterone levels? You must be joking! I've got the stuff coming out of my fuckin' ears!"

Turning away from him with another sigh, Lyn closed her eyes again and looked forward to the blessed relief of sleep.

"We'll be ok. Millions of other middle aged couples have to go through this. Why should we be any different?"

"Millions of women take HRT."

"It only delays menopausal symptoms; it doesn't stop them, and with Mum and Carrie both dead at 52, please don't expect *me* to take it."

"If you were going to get breast cancer, you'd have got it by now."

"Not necessarily, and I don't want to help it along either by taking hormones."

She felt disappointed at her husband's lack of understanding.

"I love you. Don't let this problem come between us."

"It doesn't sound as though I'm going to come at all."

"Oh, for God's sake! It's all right for you; your body still works as it should! Not only do I now have no vagina, I'm also suffering with those hot flushes you so kindly mentioned, and achy joints."

"Your choice."

"I don't have any say in it. Welcome to my world." Lyn buried herself under the duvet, incensed that the irritation she felt for her husband at that moment would probably keep her awake for the next few hours.

As the sound of snoring permeated the room a light bulb came on in her brain, causing her to sit up in bed with the consequence of her new-found realisation.

Of course! Now she knew the reason why some men seemed to have mid-life crises in their fifties and dump their ageing wives for younger women! These terrible temptresses obviously all possessed one thing...........a wonderfully oiled and functioning vagina that was not all dried up!

CHAPTER 2

THE FILLET STEAKS were frying nicely in the pan, and the jacket potatoes were making good progress in the oven. Lyn grated some cheese, and then turned the heat up under the saucepan containing two large beef tomatoes until they began to simmer.

Smoothing down the halter necked dress that she had purchased earlier that day for the occasion, she took a moment to check her appearance in a small upright mirror standing on the kitchen windowsill. Although she hated her slightly overweight body, she felt womanly and pretty as she patted a stray strand of hair into place, marvelling at how a few artful coats of paint could help her forget the march of time; her hair was now definitely blonder than it had ever been in her twenties.

She smiled at herself, trying not to notice the laughter lines etched around her eyes, and the deep ridges that had somehow formed on either side of her thinning lips. *Neil often assured her that she was still beautiful.* Lyn pursed her lips and gave her reflection a kiss before moving back towards the Aga.

Her phone buzzed on the breakfast bar with an incoming text. With a *tut* of annoyance she turned over the steaks once more, wiped her hands on a piece of kitchen paper, and picked up the phone to read the message:

'Will be late. Urgent order. Customer won't wait. X'

Lyn took a deep breath as a wave of anger washed over her: *What a cheek this late on a Friday night! The steaks were not going to wait, so the bloody customer could go and hang himself!*

She tapped into the contacts section on her iPhone and selected her husband's number. Almost immediately she could hear an irritating robotic female voice informing her that the number she had dialled was not currently available.

He had just sent her a text!

Almost growling with frustration she called the number again and then once more, but the same message was relayed back.

Could he be in an area with no signal? But then if he was, how could he have sent a text?

An acrid aroma filled the kitchen; the steaks had started to burn. She threw the phone back down onto the breakfast bar and removed the frying pan from the hotplate. The tomatoes had simmered for far too long and were now rather on the soggy side. A familiar hot flush started creeping up from her chest, causing her face to change to the same colour as the tomatoes, and her heart to race as though she had just run a marathon. A sweat broke out on her forehead and started to drip down onto her cheeks.

The heat in the kitchen was intense. Throwing off her dress she sat in her bra and knickers eating steak and potato, thinking about anniversaries past, and all the while wondering where on earth her husband had got to.

Later on there was nothing to watch on the television. She writhed around under the bedclothes in frustration, hot and bothered and unable to sleep. Hearing a key turning in the lock some three hours later, she grabbed her dressing gown, climbed out from under the duvet, and padded downstairs in her bare feet.

"Why are you so late? I hope you've eaten, because I threw your dinner in the bin." Any good humour had by now melted away.

"Did I wake you? Sorry. Mickey Reeve needed rodding out."

"Who's Mickey Reeve?" Lyn's sharp eye noticed the unusual working garb of crisp white shirt and unblemished jeans.

"New customer."

"You never told me."

"You never asked."

"I'll set up the new account tomorrow."

"It's okay; I can deal with it. I've got to do the online VAT return anyway."

A familiar aroma assailed her nostrils.

"Have you been drinking?"

"I was given a beer afterwards as an extra thanks for unblocking the toilet."

"Did you forget it was our anniversary? I'd cooked steak and potatoes; your favourite."

"Shit! Sorry. I'll make it up to you tomorrow." Neil sighed as he hung up his leather jacket.

Lyn put her arms around her husband's waist and put her head on his chest:

"Happy thirty-fifth anniversary; what's left of it. There's a card for you on the dining room table." She took a deep breath in and smelt a very pleasant aftershave on his shirt that he had never used before.

"Thanks, darling. I'm so sorry. I'll nip into town tomorrow and buy you a present."

"It's jade or coral for thirty five years."

"Christ. It would be, wouldn't it!"

"How much are you going to charge him?" "Oh, I'll figure something out."

"At least double the rate for after hours and for ruining our evening."

"Yeah, sure."

CHAPTER 3

LYN TWISTED HER new jade eternity ring around and around on the third finger of her right hand as she finalised the month-end accounts. She had a sort of gut feeling that something was missing in the figures. She looked at the ring as she twirled the stone back and forth, and realised with a start what it was that had been puzzling her: *Neil had not sent any invoice to Mickey Reeve for the out-of-hours' work done on the night of their doomed anniversary dinner.*

That particular customer's name had stuck in her mind, as with one random telephone call he had unknowingly managed to ruin the whole of their special evening. Checking on the computer she could see that no new account had been set up in that name. She looked through the in-tray in case she had missed any paperwork, but there was nothing to find. She picked up the receiver and tapped in the speed dial button for her husband's mobile phone.

"What's up?" His voice was terse as he shouted over the background noise of drilling and hammering.

"I'm finishing up the month-end. Remember our anniversary night that never was? You haven't done an invoice for Mickey Reeve or set up an account."

"I forgot."

"Well, I reckon he should be charged at least one hundred and fifty pounds for an emergency call out. You were gone all evening."

"Yeah, I'll sort out the paperwork and do it." "Where's the work sheet?"

"It's in the van somewhere. I can't talk now. See you later after the gym."

Lyn sighed as she replaced the receiver, and looked up at a recent photo of them that Neil had hung on the office wall. Granted they were not Spring chickens, but considering they were in their fifties she did not think they were ageing too badly. Neil's brown hair was greying and thinning a little on top, and they both had to wear glasses for reading, but they still had all their own teeth, their marbles, and fully functioning bladders. They were smiling as though they had not a care in the world.

She looked at herself in the photo and saw how well she had managed to hide her sadness. She supposed they probably would have been grandparents by now had they produced any children of their own in their younger days, but despite the many courses of IVF motherhood had eluded her, and some time ago it had become clear to her that she was never going to enjoy hearing the patter of tiny feet.

Satisfied with the month's accounts, she logged out and switched off the computer at the end of the day. Thursday evenings were hers alone while Neil lifted weights. Stretching her arms up to the ceiling she decided to pamper herself and have a soak in the bath before cooking their meal.

She went into the bathroom, turned on the mixer tap, and added some liquid bubbles. Hot water gushed into the Jacuzzi, and the whirlpool effect whipped up the foam into mountainous ridges. Throwing off all her clothes she sank down with a sigh and closed her eyes.

As she sloshed the bubbles around with her hands she recalled their excitement when the Jacuzzi had first been delivered; how they'd had sex in the swirling waters while Bad Company had belted out *'Feel Like Making Love'*. She had been the envy of all her girlfriends then, who had told her she had it all; the handsome husband, the big house with the fluffy carpets, and one had even commented how jealous she was of the large gas barbeque taking pride of place on the outside decking. However, she could not help but notice that nowadays it seemed that Neil preferred to take a quick shower; the barbeque had turned rusty through lack of use, and she struggled to remember the last time she had enjoyed sex.

Her achy joints pummelled into submission, Lyn stepped out of the Jacuzzi and took a warm towel off the heated rail. As she dried herself the sound of the house phone ringing jolted her out of her daydream. Wrapping the towel around her she ran quickly to the bedroom and picked up the extension.

"Hello gorgeous!"

"Hi Gary. How are you?" She had recognised the voice straight away.

"I'm fine, but more to the point how's Neil?"

"What d'you mean?"

"Has he been ill? Why has he missed the last two Thursdays? It's no fun working up a sweat on me own."

"He's had a lot of work lately. I think he's just been too busy."

"Tell him from me he's getting out of condition. I tried to tell him myself, but his phone's switched off."

She could hear Gary laughing at the other end. Rubbing the back of her neck with the towel, Lyn forced a chuckle.

"I'll tell him."

"Bye, darlin'."

"Bye." She replaced the receiver with a frown.

CHAPTER 4

"THANKS FOR THESE, but it looks like a chapel of rest in here now! What's going on?"

She laughed as she placed a vase of lilies on the polished glass top of the coffee table. Their cloying scent soon permeated every fibre of the room.

"I bought my wife some flowers, that's all." Neil sat back in his favourite armchair and switched on the TV.

Lyn hated lilies. They reminded her of funerals, of death, and of all her babies that had never been born.

"Gary rang earlier. He was at the gym and said you didn't turn up."

"I did, but I got there late. I can't always finish work at five o'clock like him. I'm self-employed; I've got to go where the work is." He hopped through several channels until he found a football match, much to her annoyance.

"He said your phone was switched off."

"I didn't have any signal. What's this; the third degree?"

Pressing the mute button on the remote control, he turned his attention away from the TV and towards her. Lyn held her breath as she felt her husband's stony gaze boring into her back as she knelt in front of him at the coffee table cutting off the lilies' brown sticky stamens.

"No of course not. I just think he wanted someone to work out with."

"I'll be there next week." He switched off the mute and returned to his programme.

Breathing a sigh of relief at avoiding another argument, Lyn finished arranging the flowers and stood up. Neil had become somewhat moodier lately, and she supposed it was all her fault for not being able to have sex.

But would he want to do something that hurt so much?

"Shall we go out to Zizi's for dinner tomorrow night?" She had already booked a table earlier in the day, certain that he would agree to an evening out at his favourite restaurant.

"Er……..I've got a private job on after work; cash in hand job. Don't know what time I'll finish." He kept his eyes fixed on the screen all the while as he spoke.

"Oh." *Shit. She would have to cancel the booking.*

"I finished the month-end. We're just over twenty five thousand pounds in the black." She decided not to bring up the subject of Mickey Reeve's elusive paperwork again just at that moment.

"That's great. Thanks."

She could see he was too engrossed in the football match to pay her much attention. Going into the hallway she grabbed the keys to the van, and decided to search it herself for the worksheet of the one customer that had spoilt her month-end figures.

Paperwork was strewn haphazardly about the interior, along with screwed-up wrappers from several fast food outlets. She retrieved the Tupperware box from the dusty floor of the van that had gone missing some time ago, which still contained the remains from a past packed lunch. She cursed her husband's laissez-faire attitude at the sight of several mouldy bread crusts and rotting salad leaves inside.

She picked up a sheaf of worksheets from the passenger seat and had a quick riffle through them, but the dates were all still current. Smiling inwardly because at least she knew what she was looking for, she gathered up more loose paperwork from the floor behind the driver's seat and scoured the dates for anything that coincided with March 19th, their anniversary.

There was nothing to find. It appeared that Mickey Reeve's worksheet had not even been completed. With a sigh of irritation she replaced the papers on the floor behind Neil's seat where she had found them, but as she did so she became aware of a flimsy piece of material poking out from underneath the seat that she had missed before. It appeared transparent and pale pink in colour.

Curious as to just what it was, Lyn pushed her hand underneath the seat and was shocked to find a pair of ladies' panties, size 10. She stood on the driveway with the panties in her hands, and looked at them in disbelief. There was a pretty red rose embroidered just above the gusset on the outside, and with a searing dismay she knew beyond a shadow of a doubt that as she was a size 16 there was no way they would ever have belonged to her.

CHAPTER 5

WHAT TO DO with the panties? Lyn looked around her hastily in case one of the neighbours had seen her standing there like a retard and staring fixedly at a pair of knickers, but thankfully the coast was clear. She stuffed the panties in her pocket, locked the van, and as she hung the keys back on the hook in the hallway she was relieved to hear that the football match was still in progress.

"Any water in that kettle?" She heard Neil bellowing from the depths of his armchair.

"No." *The bastard can make his own cup of tea!*

"Ha ha. Very funny. Put the kettle on, doll."

Ignoring her husband, she went upstairs and flopped down on the bed to think. *If the panties were not hers, then to whom did they belong?* Lyn took them out of her pocket, risked a quick look inside the gusset, and wrinkled her nose in disgust. *Somebody had been wearing them not too long ago!*

It suddenly became quite clear why she could find no worksheet for Mickey Reeve. *The simple truth was that there was obviously no Mickey Reeve at all! Neil had been rodding out the owner of the pink see-through panties in the van with his own personal rod, when he should have been at home with his wife celebrating their thirty-fifth anniversary!*

The anger began to bubble away inside her, like the stirring of magma deep below the surface of the Earth's crust before the eruption of Vesuvius. Leaving the panties laid out tastefully on Neil's pillow, Lyn jumped up from the bed and found her sewing box in the chest of drawers. Taking a large pair of pinking shears, she opened her husband's side of their shared wardrobe. With great deliberation and with much satisfaction she carefully cut one leg off all his pairs of trousers that hung over the rail, not even sparing the prized leather pair that had cost him a week's wages way back when.

She then turned her attention to the shirts and jackets; one sleeve from each soon took its place upon the discarded pile of trouser legs lying forlornly on the carpet. She pulled a suitcase from the storage space above, opened her side of the wardrobe, and filled it to the brim with enough clothes to last her a few weeks.

The football match was still in full swing. Heaving the case downstairs she put her purse, mobile phone and the keys to their holiday home and new Jaguar XJ in her handbag, put on her coat and shoes, and slid out quietly through the side door to the sound of loud cheering from her husband as the ball was kicked into goal.

The Jag's engine purred quietly as she pulled off from the driveway. Driving past the Epsom racecourse, she realised with a feeling of great relief that figuratively speaking she had burned all her boats and now had no reason to attend the hated Ladies' Day. She would have had to parade around resembling a galleon in full sail, while all the time watching Neil's eyes straying to the young shapely legs in the mini-skirts and backless/frontless tops.

She felt free and strangely energised. Hearing the phone buzzing in her handbag as she joined the slip road to the M25, she turned up the volume on the CD player and sang along to Deep Purple's 'Child in Time':

'Sweet child in time,
You'll see the line,
Line that's drawn between,
Good and bad...'

By the time the blind man had started shooting at the world, the phone had gone silent. Lyn left the volume button turned up on the CD player, as Ian Gillan wailing at full pitch would block out very nicely any more sounds that might emanate from her handbag. She joined the M4 traffic heading out of London, and at junction 20 the open road of the M5 beckoned. Relaxing into the soft leather of the seat she pushed her foot down a bit harder on the accelerator, and enjoyed the response of the powerful engine obeying her commands as it sped off into the night.

Even the seagulls were asleep by the time she had negotiated the torturous A30 and had bumped along the rough, private track that ran parallel to Hayle's three golden miles of sandy beach. The Jag's suspension had taken it all in good part however, and with a sigh of relief she turned the wheels onto the driveway of the rustic two-bedroomed cottage that had been their holiday home for the past 15 years and turned off the engine, briefly closing her eyes and wallowing in the darkness and silence of the Cornish night.

CHAPTER 6

THE COTTAGE HAD been closed up since the previous October, and there was a definite chill in the air. Lyn gave silent thanks to the inventor of gas central heating, as within a short time the radiators were humming with life and there was enough hot water for a welcome shower. Not wanting to sleep in the double bed they had so recently shared, she made up one of the single beds in the spare room and sank gratefully down into the mattress, remembering to turn off her phone just at the last moment before sleep overcame her.

It was late morning by the time she was awakened by the shrill shrieking of the seagulls on the roof. She felt refreshed after the long drive, and ready to take on whatever the day was going to throw at her.

But first, a cup of coffee to start the day.

She remembered the loose, creaky floorboard at the top of the stairs. Stepping over it gingerly she went down to the kitchen and opened the first cupboard nearest the door. There was still a jar of coffee and some powdered milk and sugar left over from their last visit, and the kettle still worked when she set it to boil.

Sitting at the kitchen table and sipping the welcome mug of hot coffee, she debated whether or not to turn her phone back on, but decided against it until she had been to Tesco's for some groceries and a good breakfast. Her rumbling stomach could not be ignored, and there was not a scrap of food in the house. After washing and grabbing some jeans and a jumper out of the suitcase, she locked up the cottage and drove a couple of miles to the nearest supermarket, pleased at the dearth of shoppers compared to the usual heaving summer throng of screaming children and shrieking mothers at the checkouts.

The sausages, eggs, mushrooms, fried bread and baked beans would do nothing for her waistline, but it tasted astonishingly good. Lyn decided she needed a treat, and that the calorific content could go off to hell in a handcart.

Arriving back at the cottage after visiting the bank and transferring a sizeable amount of her husband's money from their joint account into her own, she loaded up the fridge, dusted and polished the surfaces, and ran around the rooms with the vacuum cleaner. By then the afternoon sun was peeping through the clouds, and she could feel the warmth coming in through the windows. Opening the garden door onto the concrete patio, she dragged a deckchair outside from the storage space under the stairs, sat down, lifted her face to the sun and closed her eyes.

A mental picture of her mobile phone came into her head. With a sigh she got up from the deckchair and brought her handbag out onto the patio. With great reluctance she switched on the phone, deleted the 15 new messages from her husband without reading them, and then sat back in the chair and waited.

She was just beginning to doze when the phone's shrill ringing tone brought her back to sudden reality. She knew who it was before she even picked it up.

"What do you want?"

"What on earth have you done? I've got no fucking clothes to wear!"

On hearing the anger in his voice she stifled a giggle, and felt rather relieved there were a couple of hundred miles between them.

"What have *I* done? What's more to the point is what have *you* done?" The image of the panties came back into her mind.

"I don't know what you're talking about!"

"I'm sure you do."

"Give me a clue."

"They're pink, see-through, and have a little red rose embroidered on them. Last seen on your pillow. Before that they were under the seat in your van. And no, I wasn't checking up on you, I was looking in the van for Mickey Reeve's non-existent worksheet."

There was a long silence, and then she heard her husband sigh at the other end.

"I can explain."

"Go on then."

She had a sudden terrible thought that it had all been a big misunderstanding, and that she had somehow dreadfully over-reacted.

"I've found somebody else. It's been going on for some time now, but I didn't know how to tell you."

For the briefest of moments her world stopped in its tracks. She could hear the seagulls crying overhead and the waves crashing onto the shore on the other side of the garden wall, but these everyday sounds were part of another existence; one where she had been an adored and cherished wife. Now it seemed she had been kicked out of Neil's life like an old, discarded and worn out shoe.

"Who is she?" She fought back the tears and kept her voice even. She would not give him the satisfaction of hearing her cry.

"I put in her central heating last year. We just sort of clicked."

"Do I know her?"

"No."

"The boiler is obviously not all you put in is it? You bastard!"

"Yes I know; I'm that and more." He sighed again. "You can have the house, I don't want it. You can have the car and the cottage as well. I can hear seagulls in the background; are you down at Hayle?"

She mentally kicked herself for giving her location away so easily.

"What do you care? Piss off with Miss Pink Panties and leave me alone."

"Lyn, I want a divorce. I don't love you anymore. I want to start a new life in West Wickham and move in with Janice. Hopefully we can do this amicably."

She did not want to hear any more. Activating the off switch brought the release of a river of large salty tears that flowed down her cheeks and splashed onto the patio. A hot flush seeped insidiously over her, adding to her misery.

CHAPTER 7

SHE WAS NOT sure how long she had been sitting there, but it began to turn chilly and a biting wind had started to blow around her ankles. Lyn folded up the deckchair and returned it to the under-stairs store cupboard. She looked at the clock in the hallway, which showed ten minutes to five; she had sat there in a stupor for the best part of three hours.

She was seemingly a free woman now, and able to do just exactly what she wished. However, the sudden emancipation was not giving her as much joy as she originally thought it might. She flopped down onto the sofa in the front room, and tried to get her head around her husband's recent revelations and the effect this would have on her life.

She was fifty-five years old and had never had a job outside the home since she'd been married, although did completing Neil's bookwork every month count? She did not know, but what she had worked out was that at her advanced age it would probably be almost impossible to find any sort of paying job.

What would she do for the rest of her life? She had no family to support her; her mother and sister had both died early, and her father had passed away the year before. Her one remaining aunt was elderly and in a care home. She supposed the luxurious lifestyle would certainly have to go, along with the health club membership card, the long lunches out with friends, and the frequent holidays abroad. She was to all intents and purposes a single woman now, without an income, without a man, and taking her non-working vagina and non-existent sex drive into account, without any means to attract another one.

She put her head in her hands and wept again at the thought of going back to the vast house in Epsom with its cold king-sized bed and silent rooms, and having to be the object of cosy-couple neighbours' pitying glances. However, as she reached for a tissue to wipe her eyes, it was as if a light bulb had suddenly been turned on in her brain:

Of course! She could stay where she was and rent out the house in Epsom to paying tenants! All the cottages along the private road in Hayle were second holiday homes, and people staying in the nearby properties knew nothing at all about her. She would have a reasonable income every month if she was careful, and would be able to live anonymously in Cornwall amongst the tourists and holidaymakers in the summer, and in blissful peace and quiet throughout the winter. She could even have a go at trying to find some sort of summer job if she was bored!

Feeling somewhat pleased with herself at thinking of a solution to her problem so soon, she rose from the settee and bustled about the kitchen preparing an evening meal. She had always loved the cottage and the wild, rugged Cornish landscape. She would travel back to Epsom in a few days to pack up the house, and to sort out which items to have sent down to the cottage. She would also make an appointment to see a solicitor in order to draw up divorce papers and compose a tenant contract. It was suddenly all systems go again.

She ate happily, and when sinking into bed later that evening she thanked her lucky stars that there was also no reason anymore to have to pretend that she either wanted or enjoyed the sexual act. That was one aspect of her life she was pleased to be able to close the door on for good.

CHAPTER 8

SHE WAS AWAKE at her usual early hour, eager to greet the new day. The sun was up after breakfast, and she decided to take a walk along the beach. Grabbing her coat and scarf from the hook behind the front door, she strode out briskly into the crisp morning.

The path that led down to the sea was damp with the morning dew. Boarded-up ice cream kiosks and abandoned stripy huts along the beach below told her the new season had not yet begun.

Good; that's how she preferred it.

She nodded to a couple of dog-walkers, but otherwise she was pleased to be left alone.

The tide was receding, and there was a firm stretch of wet sand where the sea had been. She walked down close to the shoreline, felt the cold wind on her face, and thought about life being hers for the taking if she was just brave enough to venture out from under her stone.

For the last 35 years she had eschewed a career to be a loyal wife and undergo years of futile IVF treatment, and to look after Neil and support him in his business, but obviously now her services were no longer required. She may have been passed over for a younger woman, but at least she had been able to keep the house and the car, and before the day was out she would have her own current account as well, shored up with a good deal more of Neil's earnings to which she was thankfully a signatory. There was no use in thinking depressing thoughts about being dumped; she had to look on the positive side......she was free!

A seagull flew above her head, dipping and swirling in the eddies and currents. The bird's movements were mesmerising; graceful and effortless, and for a fleeting moment Lyn wished she could soar unfettered into the sky and disappear to some far off land where the sun was always shining and nobody ever grew old and past their sell-by date.

She pulled her coat around her a little tighter in the stiff breeze, and carried on walking along the sand, lost in her thoughts and not really noticing how time was passing. When she spied the Godrevy lighthouse in the distance she realised she must have walked a couple of miles at least. Feeling better for the exercise, she turned around again and started for home.

The rocky path back up to the cottage was now not so wet and slippery. Tiring just a little but still sure-footed despite not being in the first flush of youth, Lyn trod with care, but then stopped short on catching sight of a white van sitting on the driveway that had not been there earlier. She read the all-too-familiar lettering on the side with disbelief, and her good mood quickly dissipated into the salty air.

Neil Fuller: Heating and Plumbing Engineer.
www.neilkfullersplumbing.co.uk 01737 429001'

CHAPTER 9

THE AROMA OF frying bacon assailed her nostrils as she turned the key in the lock. She gave a *tut* of annoyance.

Bloody cheek!

"What are you doing here?" She felt a hot flush starting as she strode into the kitchen, not even stopping to hang up her coat. "That's my bacon!"

"Sorry, but I've been driving for hours. I'm starving."

She sweated and glared at her husband as he ate a slice of toast and stirred four rashers around in the frying pan with a fork.

"Buy your own sodding bacon!"

"I haven't come all the way down here to argue about bacon. I've come to make sure you're alright. I'm not a totally heartless bastard you know." Neil put the rashers in between two more slices of toast. "Have you got any tomato sauce?"

"No, I only ever bought it for you. Of course I'm alright! Did you expect to find some whimpering, blubbering wreck then?"

"I just wanted to know you're okay, that's all."

"I've never been better." The lie came easily. "I'll need your set of keys. This is my home now. You can't just waltz in and out as you like with Miss Pinky Pants and take over."

"Janice."

"Janice, then." She held out her arm and wiggled her fingers. "Hand them over."

She watched as he took another bite of his bacon sandwich, and then placed it half-eaten on the breakfast bar in order to remove a key from his sizeable key ring.

"Here you are. I'll phone next time."

"Thanks. New jeans?" She noticed the unusual trendy bootleg cut.

"My old ones have only got one leg."

"You don't say?" She felt the flush receding. She took off her coat and placed it on one of the kitchen stools.

"Are you going to sell the house in Epsom then?" His voice kept its even tone.

Watching him standing nonchalantly in *her* kitchen, chomping on *her* bacon, while all the time thinking of ways to dissolve their 35 year marriage so he could go off to live with his mistress made her want to pitch forward and grab him by the throat. She managed to conceal her emotions as best she could, as she placed the frying pan in the sink to soak.

"I'm going to rent it out. It'll give me an income. You've already got one; I haven't."

"It's a good idea. I was going to suggest that. Get a tenant agreement drawn up."

"I'm going to find a solicitor to do that, and I'll file for divorce while I'm at it."

Lyn felt the silence was suddenly almost palpable. Finally her husband moved over to the kettle and switched it on.

"Fine. I know it's all my fault. Go ahead and start the ball rolling. I'll have probably already done whatever it is you accuse me of." His voice took on a softer note.

"Let me know what you want from the house. I'll tell the removal men to pack it up and you can have it sent on." She swirled the scourer around the pan a little too forcefully.

"Just the stuff in the office and the tools in the shed. You can have the rest or sell it; whatever you want. Here's the address where I'm living now." He scribbled on a piece of scrap paper.

She was glad her back was turned as she read the address, so that he could not see the new tears stinging her eyes:

"I get the feeling you want me to go." He stirred a spoon in a mug of black coffee.

"It's probably best that you do. If you think I'm going to beg you to stay, you've got another think coming." She turned her head again briefly. "Go on, take the milk out of the fridge. I know you don't like black coffee." She sighed as she briskly dried the frying pan.

"Take this for the bacon." He laid fifty pounds on the table.

"Jesus. It didn't cost that much." She sniffed and kept her eyes on the crisp banknotes.

"If you're struggling for money let me know. Divorced or not, I won't let you starve."

"I'm going to take on a new lease of life. I'm going to look for work, and who knows, I might even find Mr Right at last."

She uttered the last sentence with as much bluff as she could muster. Unfortunately she was aware just as he was, that there was as much chance of her finding both as a pork chop getting into a synagogue.

CHAPTER 10

WHERE DID SHE begin to pack up 35 years of married life? On the day she started divorce proceedings she walked into the bedroom they had shared. With some relief she noticed the pink panties had disappeared from his pillow, but the single sleeves and trouser legs with their jagged edges still lay where they had fallen during her maniacal massacre with the pinking shears.

Unravelling a roll of black bin liners, she tore one off and picked up the remnants of her soon-to-be ex-husband's past life from the floor; a sleeve from the shirt she had cried on when their final IVF treatment had failed, a part of the pair of jeans he had worn on their last happy holiday in Barbados before her vagina was redundant, and half of the grey silk tie which he had kept in a box with their now mangled marriage certificate since their wedding day. When the floor was cleared she pulled the rest of the damaged clothing off the hangers and felt a strange calmness as she reunited shirts with severed sleeves and trousers with amputated legs.

The large Skip on the front lawn was soon filled with unwanted detritus from cupboards, shelves and drawers. Lyn spent the following days walking around each room writing instructions for the removal firm, and sometimes panicking slightly when it came into her head to wonder what she should do next when there was nothing more to sort out or pack up.

The office where she had worked for years on Neil's accounts had now reverted to its original purpose of a bedroom. She had got in touch with the local estate agent, had interviewed several likely tenants, and had settled on the very fertile and friendly Mr and Mrs Denney and their five boisterous children. She imagined one of the smaller Denneys probably moving in and sitting at a new desk in what used to be her work space, completing their homework or browsing the Internet. She imagined the upstairs landing would most likely soon be reverberating with iPhones, MP3's, and CD players of the young people and their friends.

The house needed children. It was too silent.

Finally, the dreaded day came when there was nothing left to organise. She looked through the big bay window in the sitting room as the removals lorry backed up the driveway, its rear sensors bleeping over the sound of birdsong on the front lawn. She did not need to have a last check around the rooms, because she knew she could always come back and live there if she wanted to when the tenants' contract expired after six months. *It was not her last ever glimpse of the house.*

She put the kettle on to boil to make the men a hot drink; an everyday action, but one that was tinged with sadness. She remembered how sometimes Neil would kiss the back of her neck as she stood there making coffee. As she added sugar to the cups she recalled the day when the coffee had turned cold by the time they had finished making love on the kitchen floor. *Now he was kissing Miss Pink Panties' neck and making love to her.....*

The removal men worked quickly and with great efficiency. She busied herself washing the cups while they loaded part of Neil into the back of the lorry; the only part she would be able to keep. When they started up the engine and moved off towards the M25 she took the spare key off the hook in the hallway to give to the estate agent, closed the front door, and rested her forehead on the cold pane of glass above the handle for one last time.

Even with the drive into Epsom to drop the key off, she was still able to overtake the lorry as it trundled along the slow lane of the M4. She felt a little more cheerful now that she had left the house behind with its brooding sadness, and sang along to Capitol Gold on the radio until the signal started to fade. By the time BBC Radio Cornwall was coming through the speakers, she had managed to retrieve a good deal of her equilibrium.

The boxes seemed to take forever to unpack, but she was pleased with the results of her labours; the house now resembled a home and looked less like a holiday cottage. She vacuumed, dusted and polished her little nest again until it shone, and took a fleeting moment to wonder whether Neil would have approved of its transformation.

CHAPTER 11

SHE LOVED THE month of May. The temperature was just right for her; not too hot and not too cold. She was getting into the habit of taking long walks along the beach, and stopping for some fruit and a bottle of water at the same little kiosk every day. Within a few short weeks she was soon on speaking terms with Sue, the kiosk's owner, who assured Lyn that she would be the first to know if any holiday jobs were going spare.

The lack of summer work and the transient nature of the local population made finding new friends particularly difficult. All the properties nearby were rented out by the week, and after a while Lyn's initial enthusiasm at greeting new faces started to evaporate when she knew that they would soon be leaving again.

When buying her weekly groceries at the supermarket she began to wonder if the checkout girl was giving her pitying looks. Meals for one and single cuts of meat suggested to her that she was marked to others as somebody who had failed in the quest to find a suitable life partner. She began wearing her wedding ring again, and tried to choose a different checkout girl each week. The ring felt somehow familiar and covered up the white indented band on her finger. After all, the divorce was not yet finalised, and so to all intents and purposes she was still married.

There was no communication from West Wickham. She wondered if Neil would feel even a little bit sad at knowing her petition for a decree nisi would soon be heard in court. Of course she knew that he had no intention of contesting the divorce, but even so they had known each other for nearly 40 years and to her it seemed similar to a bereavement; a loving husband there one day but gone the next.

She started to telephone around the friends she used to see for lunches out at the health club. They were friendly and updated her on all the gossip, but strangely enough she found there were no forthcoming invites from them to all meet up again. She pondered on this one evening, and wondered whether the women saw her as a potential threat and marriage-wrecker. She had no intention of luring anybody's husband away, but it would have been nice to have had some female company. Eventually she gave up phoning them altogether.

When her decree absolute plopped onto the doormat the beach was crowded with shrieking holidaymaking families and her morning walks had lost their allure. She took off her wedding ring and sobbed with the knowledge that she was now a single woman. That same evening, all cried out, she decided to venture out for some fresh air while the families were bathing and feeding, but then had to contend with the sight of young courting couples with their arms around each other, blissfully unaware of the pitfalls of middle age. She looked at the bare ring finger of her left hand and longed for wintertime when the beach would be hers again, but she also realised that she was also longing for some sort of companion; not for sex, but just for some human contact and the odd night out.

The solution to her loneliness stared her in the face while she watched a TV programme a few days' later. She sometimes got up to make a cup of tea during the adverts, but as she rose to her feet after part one of a particularly good drama her eyes were still fixed on the screen, which was showing yet another advert for MatchULike, the well-known nationwide dating agency. In the past she had always considered that people must be terribly ugly or really desperate to have to take up Internet dating, but now in her new life as a single woman she came to the conclusion that perhaps it was not so bad after all.

She was a normal person who had suffered a misfortune. There would probably be millions of similar souls out there who were either single and after a life partner, or like her had gone through a divorce and were now looking for companionship.

Part two of the drama was not as riveting as the thought of meeting a like-minded person at MatchULike. With a racing heart she sipped her cup of tea, and then in one fluid moment reached for her iPad, pressed the Safari button, and typed the name of the agency into the search engine. Within seconds she could see a happy smiling couple on their wedding day in front of her who had found each other through joining the site. She read of the advanced search options of filtering potential matches through personality characteristics, location, appearance and hobbies, and of particular interest to her was the statement that not everybody was looking for love; some people just wanted a friend for nights out. She read the last statement a second time; she could be matched up with a man who did not want sex!

Was there such a person? Lyn fervently hoped so. Turning off the TV, she registered quickly and paid the required fee before she had a chance to change her mind, and was soon prompted to complete a profile. The part about adding a recent photo she could have done without, but then what man searching the site would want to click on a blank face?

She would have to take a photo of herself with her iPad.

Locating the camera setting she held the iPad at arm's length, smiled her most dazzling smile, and pressed the button. Immediately a grimacing and constipated-looking gargoyle with overflow grinned back. Horrified, she pressed the delete button and tried again, only to see features resembling those of a crazed lunatic on steroids who had escaped from a mental asylum. She giggled and endured eight more disasters before securing a picture passable enough to potentially attract non-sexual companions. With a sign of relief she uploaded it into her profile page, and scrolled down quickly to the next section.

After typing in her location she decided on the false name of Greta Matthews. Her mother had often mentioned the film star Greta Garbo, who always wanted to be alone. Lyn was alone through no fault of her own, and Greta seemed a fitting *alter ego* for herself. Reading down her list of interests, Greta liked long walks along deserted beaches, visits to the cinema, meals out, and live concerts. She thought Greta sounded quite fun to be with, and then the thought struck her that if it was only companionship she was after, then another woman who also liked these interests would do just as well as any man.

The carriage clock had chimed midnight some time ago. Lyn yawned and glanced through the completed profile one last time:

'Greta Matthews is a 55 year old divorcee with no children. She lives in Hayle, Cornwall, and is a retired accountant. She is looking for men or women of a similar age for companionship, who have a sense of humour and like walking to keep fit, going out to restaurants, the theatre or cinema, and who also like rock music (preferably Seventies' bands) and live shows. Greta has blonde hair and hazel eyes.'

She had stretched the bit about being a retired accountant, and the hair was blonde only after a good coat of paint, but otherwise the rest of it was true enough. She pressed the 'submit' button and hoped for the best.

CHAPTER 12

HE MUST HAVE been at least 75 years of age and half her size. As he walked stiffly towards her she noticed the obvious dark toupee perched precariously atop sparse tufting grey hair sticking out at the sides of a head not dissimilar to a shrivelled up walnut.

"Are you Greta? I'm Terry, but you can call me Tel." He coughed violently, as her heart sank into the depths of her Jimmy Choo boots.

"Nice to meet you, Tel." Lyn forced a smile and wondered as to the best way of cutting the evening short.

"You look just like your photo."

She noticed the surprised tone of his voice, and realised that she had been just a little too trusting.

"You don't." She wondered if it had been his son or perhaps even his grandson posing for the picture.

"Oh....er......it was taken a while back."   He coughed again.

"I see."

Yeah......at least thirty five years......

"Can I get you a drink?"

"Brandy and coke please." *Will your pension stretch that far?*

"Blimey; a lady with expensive tastes."

"Oh yes; that's me." She noticed with irritation how his bottom dentures rattled as he spoke. She forced another grin and re-crossed her legs.

The bar was almost empty at such an early hour. Lyn searched around in desperation for another couple to join up with, but sadly she could see only one old man sitting alone in the corner and sipping contentedly on his pint. Looking at him she came to the conclusion that he had probably been sitting in that same seat for fifty years or more. She looked away as he lifted his glass and winked.

"One brandy and coke for the lady."

"Thanks." She took the glass from Terry's trembling hand and downed it in one.

"Fucking hell. You can't half drink!"

"I'm an alcoholic. Once I get the taste I can't stop."

"You don't say."

"Yeah. They try and dry me out at rehab, but it's no use."

As the brandy seeped into her bloodstream she felt a familiar hot flush rising from her chest.

"Your face is alight."

"Yeah. It's the menopause. I'm sweating for England now."

She noticed him eyeing up the exit as he drank his beer in record time.

"My round. I need another fix. What'll you have?" She stood up and fumbled in her purse.

"Just a half for me."

"Back in a mo. I'm just going to the loo. I'll get you another drink when I come out."

She had to stop herself from running away too fast. Opening the door to one of the cubicles she went in, sat on the toilet and closed her eyes in relief, leaning her forehead against the cool metal of the lavatory wall as she silently prayed for twenty minutes to find a way of ridding herself of the gnome-like Terry.

Finally she could not put off the evil moment any longer. Making a last adjustment to her clothing she opened the door and stepped out into the main bar area, feeling a sudden warm glow of happiness at noticing why the orange blinking lights of the fruit machines had failed to entice a single customer. *The bar was empty!* Even the old man in the corner had disappeared. Lyn felt like dancing for joy.

"Has he stood you up, love?" The barman smiled as he wiped a glass and hung it up above the counter.

"Yes thank the Lord, and ain't life grand!" Feeling as light as air, she virtually skipped all the way home.

CHAPTER 13

WITHIN A FEW days another message alert had appeared from MatchULike, and Lyn opened the email with trepidation. Working on the 'once bitten twice shy' adage, she decided not to take too much notice of the photo showing a middle aged man with a round boyish face and short spiky grey hair. Jamie Haskins was 51, had lived in Hayle for 20 years, and was into cars, motorbikes, hiking, visits to the cinema, and heavy metal. He was looking for friendship and evenings out.

Jamie certainly did not appear to be as ancient as Terry, but as she had learned to her cost, initial appearances could be deceptive. However, Lyn rather liked the look of him; he was clean-shaven with high cheekbones, and looked as if he enjoyed a bit of a laugh. She read his profile again, and decided she would definitely reply to the email.

Lyn dressed smartly for their first meeting at the local cinema. There was a good film on, but she had never before had the courage to go there alone. She was happy as she parked the car, and thought how pleasant it would be to have a companion for the evening; somebody with whom she could discuss the film afterwards before going their separate ways.

He was already outside waiting for her; slightly taller and plumper than she had imagined, but with a beaming grin and welcoming wave that put her at ease almost immediately.

"Hi Greta! Glad you could make it. Nice to meet you!"

To her ears his voice sounded a little high-pitched in timbre. She shook his hand, which felt warm and unusually soft. Lyn looked into sparkling blue eyes trimmed with long dark lashes.

"Hi Jamie! Sorry I'm a bit late; I couldn't find anywhere to park."

"No worries. I think we've still got time to get a quick drink before the film starts."

"Okay."

She followed behind as he made his way to the small crowded bar in the corner of the cinema's foyer.

"What'll it be?" He held up his hand to attract the attention of the barman.

"Oh, just a coke will be fine." She remembered just at the last moment how alcohol played havoc with her hot flushes.

"A pint and a coke please." He looked down at her. "You're cheap to take out!" He laughed as he reached out to take a drink from the barman.

"It's not unknown for me to ask for some brandy in it though, but I'll let you off tonight."

"Cheers." He raised his glass. "What shall we drink to?"

"To friendship." Lyn smiled and raised her glass.

"Yeah. To friendship."

The film was one of the best she had seen in a long time. At one point she was aware of Jamie's arm across the back of her seat, but by the time the credits were rolling and she was back in reality she was relieved to find that the arm had been removed.

"Wow. I loved that film!" Lyn stood up and gathered up her bag and jacket.

"I would say the 1974 version was better." Jamie yawned. "Mia Farrow was exquisite."

"Oh. I never saw that one." She lengthened her stride to keep up as Jamie walked quickly to the exit.

"I've got the video back at my place. You should come round and watch it".

"Sure. That sounds good."

"We could have the re-run tomorrow night if you like. Give me time to get home from work and I'll cook us some spag bol as well."

"Where do you work?"

"I'm a long-distance lorry driver, but won't be too late tomorrow because I've only got to go to Exeter."

Lyn ignored faint warning bells sounding in her head. Jamie seemed harmless enough, and she was starved of human contact.

"Okay. What time?"

"About seven. My place is next door to the fish and chip shop on Marine Parade."

"Ah yes, I know where that is. We could nip out for some chips then."

"Nah. That's my brother who does the cooking. I think he fries 'em in engine oil. You'll have the squits for a week."

Lyn laughed as she got back into her car. "See you tomorrow then Jamie."

"Yeah. Thanks for coming along." "No problem."

She took her time getting ready the following evening. She felt good; it was great to have found a new friend so soon. Lyn parked the Jag a little way down from *The Cod Father – We can batter anything!* fish and chip shop, walked back to the small one-up-one-down Victorian terraced house next to it, and rang the bell. A similar-looking but younger version of Jamie popped his head around the door of the chip shop.

"Sorry love, but Jamie's not back from work yet. She won't be long though."

She?

"Pardon? Were you talking about Jamie?" Lyn felt slightly uneasy, but could not quite put her finger on the reason why, and wondered if she had heard right.

"Yeah. She'll be about another 15 minutes. She just sent me a text to say you might turn up. Come in and wait if you like."

"It's okay. I've got to make a phone call anyway. I'll be in the car."

"Suit yourself."

The Jamie lookalike disappeared back into the shop presumably to fry his cod and pollock, leaving Lyn standing in the street open-mouthed and numb with shock.

CHAPTER 14

SHE FELT GUILTY for leaving in the way that she had. Jamie probably now had more spaghetti Bolognese than he/she knew what to do with. Lyn was ravenously hungry; she had saved herself for Jamie's pasta meal, but now had to cook something herself because she was too much of a coward to go back again.

Were there any genuinely truthful people out there in MatchULike land? How could somebody lie about something as basic as which sex they were? In the light of recent events she had even forgiven Terry for lying about his age; at least she could see that he had been a man, albeit a rather ancient one.

The Cod Father and its battering of anything came into her mind. As she put a piece of frozen haddock and some oven chips into the Aga to cook, her conscience started to remind her that she too had lied; Greta Matthews did not really exist at all, and that she was as much to blame as anybody else.

She sighed and bustled about the kitchen setting the table and making a cup of tea to go with her solitary meal. She had just raised a forkful of fish to her lips when the telephone's shrill insistence disturbed her peace and quiet. She picked up the cordless phone and gave a *tut* of irritation when noticing the number on the display screen.

"I called earlier and you weren't
in." "I was out visiting a friend."
"Male or female?" "A bit of both."

"Eh?"
"Neil; what do you want? My dinner's getting cold."
"Sorry. I just wanted to ask a favour." "Well, ask
then."
"Do you fancy carrying on doing my month-ends and tax returns?"

"You've got to be joking surely?" She put down her knife and fork and stared at the phone for a moment in amazement.

"No; perfectly serious. I'm trying to keep the costs down."

"Get Pink Knickers to do it then. She's cheap enough I expect."
"Ha ha, very funny. She can't do that sort of thing."
"What a shame."
"Ok. Never mind. Are you alright?"
"I'm fine."
"I'll pay you if you change your mind."
"I won't."
"Bye then."
"Bye."

Anger and the start of another hot tropical moment had ruined her appetite, and the chips had turned cold and soggy to boot. She finished up the haddock, threw the rest of the dinner in the bin, and washed up the plate and cutlery.

The evening stretched out before her, long and lonesome. She switched on the computer and logged in to MatchULike with the intention of browsing interesting new profiles, and sent a quick introductory hello to a pleasant looking silver-haired man of about 60 years of age, a Peter Davies, who was seeking new friends and new experiences. She then checked her inbox; there was one message alert.

'Hi Greta, What happened to you tonight? I had to eat 2 spag bols and I'm as sick as a parrot.

Ed said you'd been round. I can only assume that perhaps he'd given the game away again? I've been trying to live as a man for about a year now. However, my brother sometimes forgets if he's talking to someone but thinking about how many jars of gherkins to buy next week at the same time.

Don't let my gender issues put you off. As I said on MatchULike, I'm only after friendship. You're not my type, but it'd be great to have another evening out sometime.

Jamie x'

A gut-wrenching guilt washed over her that would not go away. She hit the 'reply' button and began to type.

'Hi Jamie, I'm so sorry. I'll admit I was shocked, as I would never have thought you were female. But I'm just as bad; I realise that I've lied as well. My name is really Lyn Fuller; I'm divorced and am also just looking for friendship and evenings out. Can we start again please?

Is there another showing of the Mia Farrow film?
Lyn x'

She hated the name Greta; it sounded old and fusty. She thought twice about adding the kiss at the bottom, but in the end left it where it was. She felt relieved as she altered her profile to show her real name, and then feeling a good deal happier she switched off the computer.

CHAPTER 15

"I WAS HOPING you'd stop by this morning. Maureen in the tea shop next door is looking for somebody to make sandwiches and salads for the rest of the season. Her girl's gone off with a surfer from Darlington."

"Thanks, Sue." Lyn handed over some coins for her usual banana and bottle of water. "I'll go in and see her."

The summer sun beat down, and the seagulls weaved convoluted whirls over her head as Lyn sat contentedly on the sea wall, watching the waves and eating her fruit. Things were looking up; she had received a reply from Jamie inviting her around again, and now there was the added promise of a little job to fill the emptiness of her days.

Most of the tables in the tea room were taken when she entered. Parents were shouting at sobbing children, and quiet older couples threw knowledgeable looks at each other. Lyn could see an older lady serving behind the counter, presumably Maureen, who appeared a little frazzled around the edges.

"Sue sent me. She said you're looking for some help."

"When can you start? I'm on my own here." Maureen wiped a bead of sweat from her forehead.

"How about right now?" Lyn smiled.

"You'll do just nicely. Hours are ten 'til four Monday to Friday, with half an hour for lunch. I have a weekend girl that comes in. Usually it'll be making sandwiches and rolls or toasted teacakes in the kitchen and keeping the counter shelves supplied. All the stuff is in a big fridge out the back. Pay is five pounds an hour; take it or leave it."

"I'll take it."

"Good! I'll show you where everything is. What's your name?"

"Lyn."

"Mine's Maureen. I'll take your details later. Right now I need four cheese and tomato rolls, and two pieces of coffee and walnut cake."

"Coming right up."

She enjoyed the baptism of fire, and the chance to prove her worth. By the end of the day her legs ached and her feet were sore, but Lyn found she liked working under pressure. All the customers had been served relatively quickly, and Maureen had a big grin on her face.

"You're a little treasure you are! Where do you live?"

"About half an hour's walk from here, in Prospect Road."

"Ah. You're local then."

"Yes."

"Wonderful! I realised too late that the other young girl was just working here until she found a fella. As soon as she did, off she went. I prefer somebody like you; more mature, and somebody who's been through all that and come out the other side."

"Oh yes; I've been through 'all that' alright." Lyn smiled and noticed Maureen looking at her left hand. "I'm divorced, but am definitely not looking for a fella."

"They all say that."

"I mean it."

"Well, it's none of my business anyway, but thanks for your help today. See you tomorrow."

She walked back home slowly along the beach. The families had all packed up for the day, and the sands were empty except for trails of footprints. She sat on a rock and rested, enjoying the time alone and the chance to wind down.

She felt as happy as a pig in the brown stuff.

CHAPTER 16

"BEFORE YOU ASK, a kind doctor did me a double mastectomy and a hysterectomy last year after three counsellors tried to talk me out of it. I told them how could I be a man with periods and size 42GG bazoomas? Oh, and the 'other' operation will be quite soon now thank God." Jamie heaped spaghetti onto two plates and poured on a thick savoury sauce.

"Wasn't that rather drastic?" Lyn did not know whether to laugh or not as she took a steaming plate. She wondered what the 'other' operation entailed, but decided not to pursue it.

"I've never been happier. I'm not female you see. I started testosterone injections some time ago and I can sing tenor in the church choir now, but not basso profundo yet. They seem to have accepted me there anyway. Unfortunately I was given a woman's body, but I'm a man inside. People tend to run away when they find out, but I'm glad you agreed on the re-run. Bon appetit."

Lyn took some Parmesan cheese from the coffee table, and then shuffled back on the settee with her tray of food.

"I'm looking forward to seeing the original version."

"Yeah. Mia Farrow looks like an angel; all frills and white lace. I've got the DVD now." Jamie switched on the TV. "You'll probably go for Robert Redford though. All the women do."

"Oh yes; he's lovely. I didn't realise he was in it."

"Prepare to be amazed. Especially when he wears his pink suit."

She felt comfortable and at ease with Jamie as they ate together and watched the trailers.

"Does your brother live here as well?"

"No. Ed lives in a flat next door above the shop. He's got a girlfriend, but keeps her on a long leash. She lives over in Penzance. You might see her one weekend; it depends if they've had a row or not."

"He seems very nice."

"He's always looked after me, and growing up he always bashed up any kid who took the piss out of the way I looked. I try to tell him I can look after myself now, but he doesn't listen."

"It must be lovely to have a brother. I've got nobody."

"Mum chucked me out when she found me in bed with a girl. I tried to tell her I wasn't gay, but in the end did it really matter if I was? She told me I was disgusting; my own mother. Ed stood up for me, but I struggled on my own until his mate found me a good job on the lorries. I've never looked back."

Lyn put down her knife and fork.

"My husband ran off with Miss Pink Knickers. We'd been married for thirty five years." She felt her eyes start to sting again and the beginning of another hot flush.

"Oh, I'm so sorry."

She was grateful for Jamie's quick hug.

"It's all water under the bridge now. We never had any children, but what tipped him over the edge was when I reached the menopause. As you can see, I'm having one of those hated tropical moments now. Neil wasn't keen on the new older me, and decided it was time to trade me in for a younger model."

"Bastard."

"I'm making a new life for myself though; new friends, and now a new job, but Mother Nature is cruel. She switches off your childbearing mechanisms, and says to you that because you're too old to make babies, then you don't need to feel the urge to have sex anymore."

"And you do?"

"No. That's the whole point Jamie; I don't. It's all gone; lock, stock and barrel.

All I've got left are the hot flushes and creaky joints."

"Ah. I see. You should have some of my testosterone then. If I had a penis it would have been worn down to a stub by now."

"But then I'll have a hairy chest and have to shave every day."

They giggled as the film begun.

"Thanks for inviting me. I'm having a great evening." Lyn ate the last of the spaghetti and sat back, replete.

"It gets better. Wait until you see Robert Redford in his pink suit."

CHAPTER 17

BY THE TIME she next managed to log in to MatchULike, Peter Davies had sent two messages. She read the first one with a heady feeling of excitement.

'Good afternoon Ms Fuller, and thanks for your email. I am a widower, and I live in St. Ives. I am a recently retired ex-Army Captain, so hope St. Ives is not too far away from you. Can we meet up?

Sincerely,
Peter Davies'

She liked the sound of Peter. She clicked on his next message.

'I forgot to say I am free every day now that I am retired, so could meet at any time that's convenient to you.
Sincerely,
Peter Davies'

Bugger it. Peter sounded nice, but she now had a job to go to during the week; he would have to wait until the weekend. She clicked on the 'reply' button:

'Hi Peter, Great to hear from you. I live in Hayle, so you're virtually around the corner! I work in one of the beachfront tearooms during the week, and so can only meet up on Saturday if that's ok with you?

Regards,
Lyn Fuller

Before she left for work the next day she checked her inbox on MatchULike, but there was no reply from Peter. Feeling slightly disappointed, she locked the front door and set off along the beach towards the tea room.

Although it was only 10 o'clock the customers were already pouring in, and Lyn was rushed off her feet keeping the counter supplied with a multitude of tempting fare. It was not until well after the lunchtime rush that she had a chance to sit down in the kitchen with a cup of coffee and a scone. She had barely taken a bite when Maureen's head appeared through the serving hatch.

"Sorry; I know you're taking a break, but there's someone out here asking for you."

"Asking for me? I don't know anybody!" She shook her head. Jamie had sent her a text to let her know she was away on a delivery up in Scotland, so it was definitely not her:

"He's quite insistent that I get you. He seems quite nice actually." Maureen gave a little smile. "I wouldn't mind it if he was asking for me."

"He must be mistaken, unless it's my ex-husband, but Neil doesn't know where I work."

"He's mentioned you by name."

Lyn took a sip of coffee, carried the cup through to the café, and came face to face with a pleasant looking silver-haired man, smartly dressed, about 55 - 60 years of age.

"Hello Ms Fuller. I'm Peter Davies. I had some time on my hands, so I thought I'd come and seek you out. You said you lived in Hayle and worked in one of the beach tearooms, so I decided to come and find you. It was damned easy actually!" He gave a little chuckle to accentuate how pleased he was with his own detection skills.

She felt embarrassed that Maureen and the remaining customers could overhear everything that was being said, and rather perturbed by the thought that all morning Peter had obviously gone from café to café along the seafront in his quest to locate her whereabouts.

The customers were looking up at her with interest. She motioned with her coffee cup towards the door, and stepped outside out of earshot. Peter grinned conspiratorially and followed her lead:

"I thought I mentioned in my email that I was free on Saturday? Today is Thursday, and as you can see I'm at work at the moment." She hoped her voice carried just the right amount of annoyance.

"Oh yes, but I was in the area and so I thought I'd say hello so we're not actually strangers when we meet."

The smile was affable and his manner genteel. Lyn relaxed and finished off the rest of her coffee.

"Well Peter, thanks for stopping by, but I've got to get back now. As I said before, I'll see you on Saturday."

"Shall I come by and pick you up then? Where do you live Ms Fuller?"

"Call me Lyn. I'll meet you outside the fish and chip shop on Marine Parade. We can walk along to the pub near there for a drink." She thought it best not to give out her address straight away, and Ed would be there to help in an emergency even if Jamie was still away.

"OK. See you about 19 hundred hours then?"

"Eh?"

"7 o'clock on the dot."

"Fine. Bye Peter."

"Goodbye."

She watched him walk away and ignored the customers' turning heads as she walked back into the tearoom. Maureen looked at her inquisitively, but she shook her head and shrugged her shoulders.

She had all but forgotten the incident in the afternoon rush. By four o'clock she was dead on her feet and ready to call it a day. She took the last of the plates out of the dishwasher and stacked them up ready for the morning. She had just closed the curtains and gathered up her bag and jacket, when Maureen's head appeared through the serving hatch.

"That chap's outside again. I think he's waiting for you."

Ignoring the other woman's grin, Lyn peered past Maureen and through the serving hatch to see with dismay a now familiar figure squinting myopically through the leaded glass of the front bay window.

"Have you locked the door?"

"Of course. We're closed now."

"Is there a back way out of here?" Lyn's voice had taken on a slight panicky tone.

"Why? What's wrong with him?"

Lyn was aware that Maureen had picked up her distress signals.

"He gives me the creeps. I don't want him to see me."

"You know there's no other exit. We've got to go out the front way unless you want to climb out through the toilet window."

"Put the key through the letter box when you go, and tell him I went home earlier. I'll wait awhile and then creep out and lock up."

"If you're sure."

"Yes, I'm sure." She tried to sound confident and in charge of the situation, but for the first time since her divorce she wished Neil was with her. She knew she would never be able to climb out through the toilet window, but at least Neil was the devil she already knew.

She did not fancy the walk home. When she was sure the coast was clear she called for a taxi, locked the café, and quickly climbed the steep tarmac slope back up to the road above. When the taxi arrived she took one last look over her shoulder as it pulled away, but could not see anything untoward at all. She breathed a sigh of relief and felt somewhat foolish at her actions, but reasoned it was better to be safe than sorry.

As soon as she was home she bolted the doors and closed the curtains. Switching on the computer she logged into MatchULike, but there were no messages. The inclination to seek out any more new contacts or meet Peter Davies outside Ed's chip shop was diminishing, and she decided to let things lie for the time being. She figured that Peter would soon get the message when she failed to turn up.

CHAPTER 18

SHE KEPT AN eye on the bay window at work the next day, but no silver-haired ex-Captains could be seen with their noses pressed up against the window pane. Lyn began to relax a little on the walk home, and even began to think about turning up outside 'The Cod Father' for the arranged 7pm assignation. However, an insistent voice in her head told her that Peter's actions had been perhaps a little on the strange side, and so to be safe she would be better off staying at home.

She sent a message via MatchULike to inform him that she had decided not to meet up after all. On the Saturday morning after breakfast she checked in to the website, but he had not replied. Feeling somewhat relieved she browsed several new profiles, but sent no emails of introduction. She then drove into town and underwent some retail therapy at the shopping centre, and spent a happy hour or two trying on her new purchases later on back at the cottage.

One of the Sky Plus channels was showing a good film that evening. She ate some lamb casserole left over from the night before, and settled herself in her favourite recliner chair ready for the start of the programme.

Her mobile phone began to vibrate on the coffee table. Sighing, she reached forward for the remote control, and pressed the button to pause the film. Checking the caller's name, she smiled and leaned back in the recliner to answer.

"Hey Jamie! How was the trip?"

"Just got back. Och the noo! I cannae understand a bloody word they're on about!"

"Yeah, I know what you mean. I was once in MacDonald's on Sauchiehall Street, and a terse voice behind the counter asked 'Arrrreyasettinin?' It took four goes before I realised he was asking me whether I wanted to eat in or take away!"

She could hear Jamie chuckling at the other end, but was not prepared for what came next.

"Listen. Ed's just knocked on the door. There's a chap sitting in the shop called Peter Davies, but he doesn't want to buy any fish and chips. He's asked Ed if he knows anyone by the name of Lyn Fuller. Ed knew you were a friend of mine, but he hasn't let on that he knows you. He's asking what you want him to say to the bloke. Can you speak to Ed a minute?"

Lyn sat bolt upright in the recliner.

"Tell Ed to say he doesn't know me! Ugh; he's really creepy. I contacted him on MatchULike, but then changed my mind about meeting him. He's stalking me, Jamie."

"What! The prick! Don't worry. I'll put him off and say you're going out with me now, and to back off."

"Would you do that? Thanks so much; hopefully that'll get rid of him."

"Yeah, I'll do it now. I'll put on my best butch voice and lean over him a bit threatening, like."

She giggled: "I know I'm laughing, but he's starting to worry me a bit. He's been around all the seafront cafes asking for me by name, and didn't give up until he found me. I had to hide inside the café until he'd gone the other night."

"Time for some drastic action then. Come round for a Sunday roast tomorrow about one o'clock and I'll tell you how it went."

"Great. Ok. See you tomorrow."

She tried to concentrate on the film, but all she could think about was her newly-acquired stalker. The fact that he now knew where she worked worried her greatly, and she decided she'd have to call in sick on Monday in case he came searching for her again.

CHAPTER 19

"GET STUCK IN; there's plenty more where that came from."

Lyn took a plate containing three expertly carved slices of roast beef and helped herself to a Yorkshire pudding and a selection of vegetables.

"Thanks for lunch Jamie. It always tastes better when somebody else cooks it." She bit appreciatively into a crispy roast potato.

"It'll be your turn next Sunday. I would have just got back from London, and I ain't eating Ed's fish and chips. After dinner if you like we can have a ride out on the bike if you've got a skid lid."

"I'll write down my address for you. What's a skid lid?"

"A crash helmet. Get on the bike and feel the wind in your face and all that. There's nothing else like it."

"Good God no! I've never been on the back of a bike and I've no intention of starting now."

"Shame. It's a Honda VFR 800 as well."

"Is that good or bad."

"Fucking good when you're on one."

She took a sip of a rather pleasantly dry, but full-bodied Bordeaux.

"Er….what happened to pervy Peter the other night?" She looked quizzically over at Jamie, who looked entirely nonplussed.

"Oh, him; he won't give you any more

trouble." "Why's that then?"

"I told him you were going out with me now, and that if he didn't stay away he'd end up under the causeway at St. Michael's Mount after the tide had come in."

Lyn nearly spluttered her wine all over the crisp white tablecloth as the urge to giggle became unbearable.

"What did he say to that?"

"There wasn't a lot he could say really; he got up and walked off."

"Cheers Jamie!" She lifted her glass, and when she had finished laughing she helped herself to some more roast potatoes.

"That's not all by the way. Ed got his twopenn'orth in as well."

"Oh God. What did he do?" She put down her knife and fork in anticipation.

"Ed informed him that if he wasn't going to buy any fish and chips, then he could piss off before he ended up battered and deep fried in oil. He particularly stressed the 'battered' bit." Jamie grinned as she passed over the salt shaker.

"I want to thank you for this delicious lunch and your amazing services as a minder. What about I buy you a drink down at the Godolphin Arms in Marazion this afternoon? We can walk across the causeway and have a look in the tropical gardens. Neil and I often went over there."

"Sure. I'm up for walking up to the castle as well if you like. Neil's your ex-husband I take it?"

"Yeah. The one that went off with a vagina encased in pink knickers."

"You can get a new one these days. It was on the news last week."

Lyn looked up from her plate with interest.

"A new husband?"

"Nah. A new vagina. Come to think of it, you can have mine if you like. When they turn it into a dick I'll tell 'em to give you whatever's left over."

"I'll look forward to that. Seriously though; how on earth can you get a new one?" Her friend's uplifting humour had pushed Peter Davies to the back of her mind.

"Well, there were these scientists in North Carolina I think it was. They took bits from three teenagers' fannies and grew new ones in a lab. I kid you not. All three girls reported that the fannies were incredible and worked just like the real thing." Jamie took a sip of wine. "There's your answer then; get down to North Carolina pronto and drop your drawers."

Lyn tried to chew but was laughing too much.

"You've missed the point. Those scientists chose teenagers. They wouldn't be able to do much with someone old like me who is dried up, has a low level of oestrogen, and can't take HRT."

"Oh well, it's a thought isn't it? Perhaps ask the doctor for a shot of oestrogen up there." Jamie grinned as she finished eating and laid her knife and fork down.

"Neil's gone and it's no use trying to get him back. No, I'm happy with the way things are at the moment." Lyn put her knife and fork to one side of the plate. "Thanks again Jamie for a lovely lunch. Let's put this lot in the dishwasher and get across the causeway before the tide comes in and pervy Pete floats to the surface."

CHAPTER 20

THE SUN WAS hot on their backs as they joined a long line of tourists walking across the cobbled path to St Michael's Mount. Lyn enjoyed the fresh breeze playing on her face and calming her hot flush, and felt a sudden gratefulness to her ex-husband for not insisting that they sell the cottage. She lifted her face to the sky and closed her eyes momentarily as she walked, and then felt Jamie giving her a slight shove.

"Keep a look out for Cormoran, in case he comes across and whisks you away."

"There's no such thing as giants. It's all a myth." She opened her eyes again and saw the castle looming closer.

"That's why you can't see any cows or sheep. He's stolen them."

"We're walking along the sea bed, Jamie; that's probably the reason why." She gave her friend a shove, knocking her off the cobbles and onto the wet sand.

"Oh yeah."

They climbed the harbour steps and joined the queue at the ticket office to gain entry to the castle and grounds.

"I'll get the tickets as a thank you for

lunch." "You've already bought me a pint."

"Thank Neil; he's very generously donating his money this afternoon." Lyn laughed as she waved the joint bank account card about.

"I've never met the bloke, and already I like him. Cheers."

"Don't like him too much though. He's a

prat." "Ok. I'll only like his debit card then."

She found that she was puffing slightly on the ascent to the castle, but to her annoyance Jamie was sprinting ahead not unlike a mountain goat.

"Stop a minute. I'm out of breath." Dazzled by the sun's rays, she gazed over the railings at the picturesque sub-tropical gardens below basking in the heat, and waited for her pounding heart to regain its normal rhythm. The seagulls screamed overhead, and looking downwards she felt as if she had somehow arrived at the top of the world. She saw Jamie start to backtrack down the steep granite steps.

"It's a lovely view. I often come up here by myself. It's better with somebody else though."

"God, I'm unfit. Can we sit on this bench for a minute?"

"Sure. The belly full of roast beef probably isn't helping."

When she felt ready they carried on up to the entrance of the castle.

"I love looking at the guns and suits of armour."

"Typical bloke. I like the peace and quiet of the little

church. Neil used to go off and leave me soaking up the spiritual energy."

Lyn realised all at once it was the first time she would visit the chapel knowing that Neil would not be coming there to seek her out and to stand there impatiently waiting to go. It was a bittersweet moment.

"No, it's a special place. I love it too. I want to start sensing invisible ley lines when I come back out and sit on the grass."

"It gets you like that, doesn't it?" She smiled; glad momentarily to be able to share in one of the last remaining vestiges of Jamie's femininity.

"Let's do a selfie by the cannons."

Lyn laughed as Jamie put an arm around her waist, switched her iPhone to the camera mode, and held the phone at arm's length.

"Would you like me to take a photo of you and your wife?" A passing tourist smiled at Jamie.

"That'll be great, thanks." Jamie handed over the phone. "You know what? You've just made my day!"

The descent was not much easier. After walking around the castle for a couple of hours she was weary, and found her thigh muscles kept threatening to go into seizure as she negotiated the steps once again and that her knee joints had started to ache.

"Can we rest a minute, Jamie? I'm sorry but my legs aren't as supple as they were the last time I did this." She flopped down onto a welcome bench with the beginning of another hot flush.

"No probs. It gets us all in the end. Here, have some of my water." She took a bottle out of her backpack.

"I don't do this often enough to have built up my muscles. Sorry."

"Shut up and enjoy the view."

They sat in silence for a while until she felt able to tackle the slope again.

"I'm ready." She stood up, hating how her legs felt weak and jelly-like.

"I'll race you across the causeway."

"No way! I'm already going to have stiff muscles tomorrow. I'll let you win."

"Spoilsport."

CHAPTER 21

AFTER THE TRIP out with Jamie, Lyn returned home pleasantly fatigued. As she turned the key in the lock she felt that at last she was starting to settle down into the Cornish way of life. She was enjoying her little job, and the upset of the divorce was beginning to fade. She had made a firm friend in Jamie, and after preparing herself a sandwich, decided it would be good thing to add even more companions to her list. Smiling at the blatant U-turn on her previous decision *(Neil always used to hate it when she kept changing her mind)*, she thought a good way of spending the evening would be to search for some more possible companions on MatchULike.

Two messages were awaiting her attention when she logged in. Clicking on the first one she read an introductory email from a Barry Simpson, who was 58, an air-con engineer, fair-skinned, of medium build, and into quiet dinners in cosy restaurants, rock festivals, going to the cinema and pub, and fly fishing. He was looking for good times with good friends.

She couldn't give two hoots about fly fishing, but the quiet dinners, festivals and cinema visits sounded ok.

Composing a suitable response took some time, but Lyn was pleased with the light-hearted result of her efforts.

'Hi Barry, thanks for the email. I'm 55, divorced with no children, and like you am also looking for good times with good friends. I've been living in Cornwall since March, and I find I'm really loving the way of life down here. If you fancy meeting up once you've read through my profile, please send me a message back.

Regards,

Lyn Fuller'

After opening the second message her heart started to beat a little bit faster in her chest.

'Good afternoon Lyn, I'd like to apologise for upsetting your boyfriend and his pal on Saturday night. I'm afraid I didn't get your message cancelling our meeting until I switched on the computer Sunday morning. It was my own fault for not logging in I suppose, but after I spoke to the unpleasant chap frying chips, all hell seemed to be let loose. I now realise you are 'taken' as it were, so please forgive me if I appeared a little too forward.

Sincerely,

Peter Davies'

She sighed as she realised her fears had been without foundation; Peter seemed nice enough. She debated whether to reply, but at the last minute decided against it. She was still perturbed at the odd way in which he had tried to find her, and came to the conclusion that with the world in the state that it was today, a girl could never be too careful. She left the reply in her inbox without answering it, and decided to throw a 'sickie' the following day in case he came looking for her at the café.

CHAPTER 22

"ARE YOU FEELING better now?" Maureen sprayed some disinfectant onto the yellow Formica tablecloth in front of her and gave it a wipe.

"Yes I'm fine. I think I must have eaten something dodgy on Sunday."

Lyn stood with bated breath to hear whether Peter Davies had made an appearance the day before. However, Maureen just carried on wiping the tables clean and humming to herself. Lyn heaved a sigh of relief and set to work, moving to and fro between the kitchen and the café, filling the refrigerated shelving under the counter with sandwiches and cakes ready for the morning rush.

The morning was a little cooler, and the customers were slow to arrive. Around 11 o'clock she signalled to Maureen that she was going to take a 15 minute break, and took a cup of coffee outside to her favourite spot by the sea wall. Swinging her legs over to the far side of the wall she sat contentedly looking out to sea and sipping the frothy latte as she watched the families frolicking down on the beach below.

"You never answered my email."

A soft voice coming from behind startled her and caused her to spill coffee down the front of her tunic. She turned her head to the left and came face to face with a smartly-dressed man aged about 60 with silver hair, who wore beige chino trousers, a pale blue polo-necked shirt, and a dark blue blazer, and who was now definitely stalking her. She noticed his outfit was finished off with white deck shoes emblazoned on one side with miniature royal blue anchors.

"Oh. Hello Peter. You made me jump!" She could not put her finger on quite why she was dismayed to see him, but dismayed she definitely was.

"Sorry to startle you. I just needed to know that things were ok between us and that you had accepted my apology."

'Of course." She wondered how long he had been watching the café and waiting for her to come out.

"I like things cut and dried. Can't have unfinished business hanging over my head."

"Absolutely. I'm the same." She wished he would go away.

"I knew we were similar in outlook."

He stood there immaculate and without a strand of slicked-down hair out of place. She looked at her watch and rose to her feet.

"Sorry Peter, but my break time is over. I have to go back to work now."

"My apologies again for disturbing you. Goodbye." He gave the slightest of bows as he turned on his heel with almost military precision.

"'Bye."

She virtually ran back into the café and closed the door to the kitchen. Almost immediately Maureen popped her head through the serving hatch.

"We could do with some more Cornish pasties please."

"I'll put some in the oven to cook."

She made her way towards the freezer, hoping that Maureen had not spied her unwelcome visitor.

"Was that the chap outside who you were hiding from last week?"

Lyn grimaced as she opened a box of uncooked pasties. Maureen was obviously as sharp as a tack.

"Yes that was pervy Peter alright. I hope I've seen the last of him now."

"He seems very nice to me. Well-mannered and the true English gent type."

"I'm sure he is. I just wish he'd go off and be a gent to somebody else."

"Send him my way. He can doff his cap to me any time."

"I'll do that." She gave a hollow laugh.

Thankfully at four o'clock the beachfront was empty of old-fashioned silver-haired English gents as she began her homeward journey. After her evening meal she logged onto MatchULike and saw a reply to her message from Barry Simpson.

'Hi Lyn, I'm free tonight. Fancy meeting up for a drink?"
Regards,
Barry'

CHAPTER 23

"DO YOU KNOW that chap in that fish shop over there?"

She followed Barry's gaze as he pointed out Ed Haskins waving at them from behind the counter of *'The Cod Father'*.

"Oh; he's the brother of a good friend of mine." Lyn waved back; glad that Ed was nearby for moral

support. "Well; where do you want to go then?"

Lyn thought that Barry sounded just a fraction irritable. She indicated towards the pub situated on the corner.

"We can go in the pub over there if you like."

"Is the barman a friend of yours as well?"

"No; is he a friend of yours?" Lyn was finding Barry's manner slightly off-putting, and had decided to ignore a hot flush and answer him in the same terse tone.

She watched as Barry visibly relaxed, smiled, and ran a hand through his obvious dyed dark brown hair:

"No. I don't know anyone around here. Come on then; I'll buy you a drink."

She walked alongside him, noticing his black pointy-toed cowboy boots, scruffy jeans, and frayed Iron Maiden t-shirt. She also noticed with some surprise a small gold sleeper-type earring in his left ear.

"What'll it be?"

She thought she had better keep her wits about her. "Just a small vodka and orange please." She sat herself down on a seat in the corner and looked at the back view of Barry as he queued up at the bar. His hair seemed overly long, but he was rather agreeably well-muscled and looked as though he would have no trouble keeping his end up in a fight.

"There you go. A small one for the lady."

"Thanks." She took the glass from a none-too-clean hand, and put it down on the table.

"Drink up, and then perhaps we can go on somewhere else."

"I'm ok here for now. Do you live nearby?" The vibes coming her way from Barry were starting to put her on her guard. She sipped her drink slowly, feigned some sort of interest, and wondered when it would be appropriate to make her escape.

"I live in Camborne, near the White Hart pub. It's my local; do you know it?" He had downed almost two thirds of a pint of bitter before she could reply.

"Not really; I've only been living down this way for a few months since my divorce."

"Divorced eh? You'll be gagging for it then." The rest of the pint disappeared and the glass was slapped back on the table.

Lyn looked aghast at Barry as he wiped his mouth with the back of his hand:

"Gagging for what?" She wondered if she had heard him right.

"You know. A bit of the other." He belched. "Another drink? You seem a bit tense."

"I'm not gagging for anything, especially not 'a bit of the other' as you put it. And no, I don't want any more to drink thanks." She crossed her legs and reached in her handbag to locate the whereabouts of her car keys.

"You birds are all the same; sending me messages saying you like a good time, and then turning out to be as frozen as a penguin's chuff."

"I apologise if I gave out the wrong signals. My idea of having a good time is obviously different from yours." She was glad to be in a crowded bar and felt reasonably safe, so decided to give the sex-mad Barry a piece of her mind.

"What else is there?" Barry stood up and looked towards the exit.

"There are lots of things to do that don't include 'a bit of the other'. Good times could be a night out at the theatre, the cinema, a club, even an evening spent in a nice pub with a view of the river or something like that." She was enjoying herself now.

"Stuff it. See ya, darlin'."

"I'm not your darling."

"Too fucking right you're not."

She followed Barry's muscly back as it disappeared out of the door, then with a sigh she relaxed, smiled, and settled back in her seat temporarily to finish her vodka and orange.

CHAPTER 24

"CHEER UP; HE could have got you pissed on double vodkas and then driven you back to his place to show you his etchings."

Lyn laughed at Jamie and placed a mountain of fried chicken, coleslaw and salad on the table.

"Is there a man alive who doesn't want sex?"

"Probably not, we're all the same; at least I will be when they give me a dick." Jamie heaped her plate high and picked up her knife and fork. "Never mind. I've brought Ed's gear and skid lid over. If they fit we're going down to Land's End this afternoon on the bike. Once you get away from the circus they've built near the car park, it's still a nice walk along the cliffs."

"You've got to be joking!" Lyn clamped her jaw shut, where it had opened wide in astonishment.

"Never more serious. You need to stop thinking about men, get into leather and straddle my VFR."

"Oh my God. No!" She lost the resolve not to giggle. However, the increasing temptation to try something new that she had never done before was suddenly overwhelming, and after lunch and a little more persuasion she decided to give it a try.

The bike seemed huge up close, and she felt slightly claustrophobic wearing the unfamiliar crash helmet. The weight of Ed's leather trousers made it difficult to lift her leg over the seat of the bike.

"Don't forget; hold on around my waist and just follow the bike; a slight swaying motion with the hips if I have to turn. Don't lean too much as we go round the bends, and don't lean the other way either, or we'll end up crashing into a bloody tree. Oh….. and no pecking."

"Eh?"

"Don't let your skid lid crash into mine if I have to put the brakes on. Peckers really piss me off!"

"I think I've changed my mind." Her heart started to pound.

"Too late! Anyway, it'll only take about half an hour to get there."

Jamie turned the key to start the engine. The sound of a throaty roar filled her with dread, as her seat began to vibrate.

"Don't you have to kick start bikes anymore?" She shouted over the noise of the throttle.

"Nah. You've been drooling over Richard Gere in 'An Officer and a Gentleman' haven't you? That film was made ages ago!"

She closed her eyes and held on for dear life, but by the time they were zooming along the A30 she had relaxed somewhat, was quite enjoying the ride, and felt confident in Jamie's ability to handle the machine. When they arrived at Land's End she felt exhilarated and quite disappointed that the journey had ended.

"You're a natural. See; I knew you'd like it!" Jamie started to thread a chain through the back wheel. "Put your skid lid on the footrest like I've done, and I'll chain them to the bike. We'll have to carry our jackets, but we can find a nice place to sit and take off the leathers for a while in a minute."

"I'm sweating already. I'm not sure if it's a hot flush, the hot weather, or the leather jacket." Lyn felt ten stones heavier in the bulky clothing.

"Yeah, it's an occupational hazard of biking in hot weather, but you don't want to come off and only have shorts and sandals on. I made that mistake when I was nineteen and silly."

"Why did you and the other bikers on the road keep nodding to each other?"

"Don't know really, but you know you're in with the in crowd if you get a nod; it's a bloke with a big bike thing. Let's walk up to the First & Last and we can get an ice cream."

"I feel like John Wayne when he got off his horse after a day in the saddle."

Lyn carried her heavy jacket and waddled alongside Jamie. "Blimey, it's changed since Neil and I came here last. There only used to be rocks to clamber over and the First and Last." She looked around surprised at the theme park that had sprung up seemingly out of nowhere.

"Yeah, it's terrible isn't it? It's like entering the gates of hell. Get past this and you'll recognise it a bit more. You can't even clamber over the rocks anymore because they're all roped off for your safety. They want you to spend money here instead." Jamie wrinkled her nose in disgust at the flashing lights all around them.

"People can't climb over the rocks now?" Lyn recalled with a stab of nostalgia what else she and Neil had done under cover of a particularly large slab of granite.

"Nope. All gone."

"What a sad day for mankind."

"I remember when Ed was about ten. He slipped on a rock and nearly went headfirst into the sea one time. I expect that's one of the reasons they were roped off; to protect small boys from killing themselves."

The First and Last café was just how she remembered it. Lyn threw Ed's jacket onto the wooden bench outside the café, and sank down gratefully whilst Jamie went inside to buy the ice creams.

"Yours is the pink one. Get your laughing gear round that." Jamie held out a strawberry cone and a bottle of water, and then plonked herself down next to Lyn.

"Great. Thanks. I think I'm melting into a puddle of molten leather." Lyn accepted the ice cream gratefully, and took a sip from the ice cold bottle.

"You'll get used to it. We can find a nice spot to sit down on the cliffs and look at the sea in a minute."

They ate in companionable silence, and after walking to a grassy knoll and divesting herself of the cumbersome leather trousers and ankle boots, Lyn sat in a state of blissful nirvana in her jeans, socks and t-shirt, looking out over the cliffs and thinking of nothing in particular whilst Jamie dozed. Later, sitting back on the bike and feeling the cooling wind through the leathers, she tried to think back to when she had enjoyed an afternoon more.

CHAPTER 25

MAUREEN POPPED HER head through the serving hatch.

"I'm going home early; I'm feeling a bit icky. Do you think you'll be okay putting the takings in the safe and locking up please? I'll give you the keys."

"Sure. No problem." Lyn smiled as she opened the door to the dishwasher, letting out a blast of hot steam.

"I'll go to the bank tomorrow. There's only two customers left. Put the blinds down when they go and get off early.

"Thanks. Will do. You get off now." Lyn emptied the dishwasher and then went into the café to wipe the tables.

She pulled down the blinds, locked the door and put up the 'closed' sign after the last couple had left. The beach was empty of holidaymakers, and rain clouds were gathering. Taking her time she counted out three hundred and forty two pounds and sixty eight pence from the till and took it to the square safe located in the wall opposite the door just above the skirting board in Maureen's tiny office. The safe was partially obscured by a desk, and she had not even noticed it was there before until Maureen had pointed it out.

She spun the combination lock, feeling relieved that the takings were secure for the night. She switched off the light, closed the office door, and then locked it with one of the keys from Maureen's key ring. Satisfied that the kitchen and café areas were clean and tidy, she turned off the main lights, grabbed her bag and jacket, and unlocked the main door.

She was thrown backwards into one of the café tables by a hand pushing hard against her ribcage. She dropped her handbag in fright; its contents scattering all over the recently swept floor. Stumbling and holding onto the table for balance, she righted herself and came face to face with a man wearing grubby combats and a balaclava, a large knife flashing menacingly in his right hand.

"Just give me the money and you won't get hurt." His eyes through the balaclava were dark; the lids hooded. He closed the door and locked it again behind him.

Lyn's legs had turned to jelly, and her heart was pounding enough to burst right out of her chest. She looked around blindly for her purse, which had fallen under the table. She picked it up and opened the clasp.

"I've not got much cash on me. I don't get paid until tomorrow." Her voice trembled in fright.

"I want today's takings. Get the money out of the till now." The tone was soft and menacing as the man advanced closer. He took her purse, looked inside, swore, and threw it back on the floor.

"Maureen took the money with her when she left. I'm not allowed to lock up and leave cash in here overnight." Her mouth felt dry as she played for time, hoping he would believe the lie; while she desperately tried to think of something she could do to end the situation. Her eyes darted about on the floor, trying to locate the whereabouts of her phone.

"Open the till."

She felt the tip of the knife touching her neck. With leaden steps she went over to the till and switched it on. It pinged open to reveal only bare compartments.

"Where's the money? Don't fuck with me!"

She felt an arm go around her neck and his stale breath in her ear as he stood behind her.

"I told you; there isn't any!" She wanted to cry as the knife in his hand hovered in front of her face. She closed her eyes and attempted to get a grip on the situation. As she fought to control her emotions, seemingly from a distance she was aware that somebody was lifting up the letter box and shouting through the opening.

"Ms Fuller; it's Peter Davies. Are you okay? I was passing, saw everything and phoned the police. I just want to let you to know that they've arrived and are surrounding the cafe. Mission accomplished."

She never thought she would be so overjoyed to hear the voice of her stalker.

She felt the grip on her neck loosening.

"Thanks Peter! I'm alright!" She shouted as loudly as she could. Her voice sounded hollow in the empty café.

"Shut the fuck up! Where's the back door?" The man's voice was less confident now and nervier.

"There isn't one." She felt more in control now, and thanked the Lord above for her good fortune.

"Then you're coming out the front with me. You're my insurance." An arm went around her neck again and the knife came in close. "Move. Go and open the blinds."

She walked slowly to the door, pulled up the blind, and came face to face with Peter Davies and three burly policemen.

"Fuck off all of you or she gets it!" The man shouted over the noise of the seagulls outside.

"This is Police Constable David Hargreaves. Drop the knife and come out! You will not get away! I repeat; you will not get away! It will be better for you if you give yourself up now!"

It seemed an eternity but was probably only about a couple of minutes; the arm relaxed around her neck, and the man unlocked the door still carrying the knife, but with his hands held up in the air.

Lyn found her legs had once more reverted to a jelly-like substance. She went back into the café and sat down with a sigh at one of the tables, as the man was led away. She smiled weakly in Peter's direction as he busied himself picking up her belongings from the floor and putting them back in her handbag.

"Glad to be of service to a damsel in distress." He held out her bag, and she took it gratefully.

"Thanks so much. What were you doing here? We close at four." She hadn't the heart to report him for possible stalking to the policewoman coming towards her.

"Oh - just passing when I saw the young chap hanging about outside. He pulled a balaclava on, and I saw him push you back into the café. I knew I'd be no match for him these days, but luckily I had my mobile with me." He waved the phone about.

"Would you be prepared to come down to the station and make a statement?" The young policewoman smiled as she looked down at Lyn." Did he take anything?"

"No. I never let on where the safe was. Yes, I'll come down and make a statement now after I've locked up." Lyn rose to her feet a little shakily, a hot flush starting to creep across her cheeks.

"We'll need you as well, Mr Davies." The policewoman checked around the café before going back outside.

"I'll be there. I'll take Ms Fuller in the car." Peter rolled the blind back down on the window.

"Do you know this man?" The policewoman glanced at Lyn questioningly and then back towards Peter.

"Sort of. It's okay Peter, I'll go with the police." Lyn did not feel like tempting fate twice in one evening.

"As you wish. I will see you at the station. Over and out." With the faintest of salutes Peter Davies gave a little bow and then marched off briskly down the Esplanade.

CHAPTER 26

Soaking in the bath at the end of the day, she had to admit to herself that Peter had behaved like a perfect gentleman throughout the couple of hours she had spent down at the police station. She had been too tired to turn down his offer of a pub meal and a lift home, but to be on the safe side she had made him drop her a short distance away from the cottage. She was still a little uncertain about his strange manner and clipped speech, but figured that a lifetime in the Army had possibly made him the way he was.

Putting on a clean track suit, she sank down on the sofa and prepared to veg out for the evening in front of the TV. However, although she felt tired, the adrenalin was still running through her system and she found it difficult to settle. Sighing, she got up and tried sipping some camomile tea, but her mind kept flashing back to the young man in the balaclava. After phoning Maureen and updating her with all that had gone on, she decided to take up her boss's offer of a couple of days off to recuperate and sent a text to confirm.

Later, lying in bed and listening to the wind in the trees outside and the old timbers in the cottage creaking and settling down for the night, her mind started to race with haphazard thoughts of intruders gaining entry and creeping up the stairs. Rising from her bed she put on her dressing gown and re-checked that the doors and windows still remained locked. Annoyed at her own foolishness, she gave up thoughts of trying to go to sleep, switched on the computer instead, and logged into MatchULike.

There was one message waiting in her inbox.

Hi Lyn, I saw your profile. If you fancy nights out and a laugh, we're looking for supporters for our rock band. Check out my blurb and get back to me if you fancy meeting up. My name's Catherine, but everyone calls me Cat. Regards, Cat Morris.

Cat was 53, and into rock and classical music, walking, going to the gym, cinema and eating out, but most of all playing guitar in her band.

Lyn decided that Cat sounded fun and was just what she was looking for; somebody near her own age who was obviously not interested in sex, and just wanted to have a laugh and a good night out. She sent a thank-you email to Peter Davies for all his help, and also a reply to Cat Morris before switching off the computer and going back upstairs.

Hi Cat, thanks for your message. It'll be great to hear your band play. I live in Hayle. Where are you? I have my own transport, so am fairly flexible where meeting up is concerned. Regards, Lyn Fuller.

On logging in the next morning she found that Cat had sent a reply almost straight away, but there was no message from Peter.

'Hi Lyn, come along to 'The Grapes' pub in Hayle on Saturday night at about 7pm. I'll be sound checking with the band. It'll be great to meet you! Cat.'

Feeling slightly apprehensive Lyn looked up the location of the pub on Google. It was over the other side of Hayle and was a venue for live music, especially featuring local unsigned bands. She scrolled down the list of bands, and checked out the name of the one playing on Saturday night. She read that 'Les Zepp' were an all-girl Led Zeppelin tribute band, consisting of Roberta Pant, Ginny Rage, Joan Bonk'em, and Les-Brianne Moans.

Joan Bonk'em and Les-Brianne Moans? She giggled and wondered which member of Led Zeppelin Cat Morris was impersonating. The photo showed four women obviously past their prime but still looking great, with good figures and big hairdos, who were pouting and posing together wearing designer distressed jeans and strappy tops.

Les-Brianne Moans? She glanced again at the women, but decided a night out at The Grapes would be just what the doctor ordered after all she had gone through.

The band were just setting up when she arrived. Slightly nervous, and wearing a new pair of jeans and a black Led Zeppelin t-shirt that she had bought from the HMV shop that afternoon, she first ordered herself a brandy and coke at the bar for courage. Taking a deep breath she then walked over towards the ordinary-looking middle-aged woman with short mousy hair, wearing cut-off jeans and a man's shirt who was adjusting controls on her amplifier.

"Hi. I'm Lyn Fuller. Which one of you is Cat Morris?" She smiled as she downed a few mouthfuls of the brandy.

"That's me for my sins. Hi!" Cat switched her guitar to her left hand and extended her right.

"Pleased to meet you Cat. I take it you're Ginny Rage then?" Lyn giggled as she shook the warm, solid hand.

"Yeah. I always wanted to be Roberta Pant, but I've got a voice like a corncrake."

"Join the club. Thanks for inviting me tonight."

"No probs. I'll introduce you to the girls, but look out for Joan Bonk'em over there." She pointed to a woman at the far end of the stage taking out cymbals from a round bag marked 'Paiste'.

"Why?"

"You'll find out soon enough." Cat laughed. "Hey girls! My new friend Lyn's come to watch us play tonight."

Lyn found that she was soon surrounded by curious, friendly women not much younger than herself.

"Nice of you to come along. I'm Sue Richards, alias Roberta Pant."

Lyn thought that Sue looked somewhere in her late forties. She had short red hair and was tall and willowy, but did not seem to resemble Robert Plant at all.

"Wait 'till you see the wig. It's the wig that does it." Sue giggled, as though reading her thoughts.

"Well, hello darling! I'm Caroline French, known as Joan Bonk'em, although I don't know why. Enchanted to meet you!"

Lyn was enveloped in a waft of perfume as Caroline kissed her on both cheeks, but she soon felt uncomfortable at being up so close to another female who had not moved backwards into her own personal space after the introductions had been accomplished. Stepping back into a more comfortable zone, she took in the woman's dark, sultry looks and long black hair.

"Nice to meet you Caroline. I can't wait to hear the band play!" Lyn moved back another step and finished off her brandy and coke. She felt the start of a hot flush that began to spread upwards from the middle of her chest until it had soon taken over the whole of her face.

"I used to get those, but I'm loaded on HRT now. Hi; I'm Denise Rogers, but I go by the delightful moniker of Les-Brianne Moans."

It was no use trying to hide her scarlet cheeks. Lyn smiled and shrugged her shoulders at a short, slightly overweight woman with shoulder length curly brown hair, holding a bass guitar nearly as big as she was.

"Hi Denise. I can't take it, but the flushes aren't nearly as bad as they used to be."

"Mine were terrible. I had to take several changes of clothes everywhere I went."

"Good God. I was never that bad." Lyn smiled and felt an instant rapport with the bass player.

"Hot flushes or not, you can shake my tambourine any time. Nice"

Lyn recoiled slightly as Caroline moved towards her again and touched the front of her t-shirt.

"Really?" Lyn wondered whether the drummer was discussing her breasts or the Led Zeppelin motif.

"Joanie, behave yourself and set up. The punters'll be here in a minute."

Lyn gave a sigh of relief as Cat ushered Caroline back over towards her drum kit. Caroline leered at her as she began to adjust the height of two cymbal stands.

"Don't take any notice of her. She hasn't had sex for a few days." Cat laughed and switched on her amplifier.

"Well, it's not worth her trying it on with me, is it?" Lyn shouted over the sounds of power chords emanating from Cat's guitar.

"She'll go after any female alive; young or old. Unfortunately for you she has a penchant for blondes, but don't worry, I'll tell her you're straight." Cat started to softly play the intro for 'Whole Lotta Love.'

"Oh shit."

"Why d'you think we're called Les Zepp?

"Thanks for the info." Lyn's heart sank down to her new Jimmy Choo's as she took a seat and wondered what she had let herself in for.

CHAPTER 27

THE PUB'S MOSTLY female audience was rocking. Clever wigs had turned three of the band members into passable substitutes of the originals. Lyn saw that all Caroline had had to do was to tie a bandana around her long black hair and to hit the drums as hard as she could. The crowd were too enthusiastic and intoxicated to bother about a change of gender.

"What are you doing here? I wouldn't have thought this was your kind of thing at all!"

She looked around with surprise at a familiar voice.

"Jamie! You're back! These are new friends from MatchULike. I've only met them this evening."

"You want to watch out for Joanie; she'll go after anything female that's breathing. She even tried it on with me once, until I told her I was a bloke. She left me alone after that, but we've been friends ever since and I usually support any local gigs the band do."

"She thinks you're a man?" Lyn resisted the urge to giggle.

"I am a man; well, apart from a small discrepancy. You thought so too as I recall" Jamie finished a pint of beer, and wiped her mouth with the back of her hand.

"You're more male than some men I know."

"Cheers for that….. MOBY DICK!!!!"   Jamie shouted and waved her arms at the drummer to attract her attention. Caroline acknowledged her friend by grinning and expertly twirling her drumsticks in the air.

Lyn recognised Denise's rendition of John-Paul Jones' slow bass build-up into the start of 'Dazed and Confused'. Cat's guitar chords kept pace, and the atmosphere was electric as the stage technician dimmed the spotlights. She saw Sue shake her long blonde wig, adopt a wider stance, wipe the sweat from her forehead, and mentally prepare herself to last the distance. Caroline waited, sticks in hand, for her cue. When Sue could be heard belting out how the 'soul of a woman is created below', Caroline nearly leapt from her drum stool, and Lyn was unprepared for the massive cheer from the crowd.

"They always do that!" Jamie laughed and jumped up and down with the audience.

"Is everyone here gay except me?" Lyn looked around at the band's supporters; mostly female couples with their arms around each other.

"You and I are probably the only ones who aren't, but I'm not bothered about it. They're just great mates of mine. MOBY DICK!!!" Jamie laughed as Caroline mouthed an unflattering word in her direction.

The one brandy would have to do as she was driving home, but Lyn found she was not need of alcohol to have a good time. The band were excellent, and as 'Rock and Roll' closed the first half of the set, she found she was jumping up and down with the rest of the audience, her arm on Jamie's shoulder.

"Put him down; you don't know where he's been!"

Lyn watched as Caroline climbed down from her drum kit and passed nearby, spitting venom as she headed straight for the bar.

"You were great, Caroline!" Lyn hated confrontations. She took her hand from Jamie's shoulder and waved it to gain the drummer's attention.

"She's sulking. I know that look anywhere. If she thinks you're with me then she knows you're straight." Jamie turned to quickly glance at Caroline queuing up at the bar.

"Oh God. I didn't come here to cause a fight."

"Take no notice of her. Did you enjoy the first half?" Cat came and sat down with a glass of lemonade.

"You're all incredible! I haven't enjoyed myself so much since the ride to Land's End on Jamie's bike." Lyn smiled at her new friends, found an empty seat next to Jamie, and sat down.

"Yeah. That was a nice day wasn't it?" Jamie belched as she finished a second pint of beer.

"I hope you're staying for the second half? We'll all hit the town afterwards and find a kebab shop that's still open, if you want to come along? Real rock 'n roll!" Cat laughed as she opened a bag of crisps.

Lyn felt relaxed and did not want the evening to end.

"Sure. Coming Jamie?"

"Why not? I'll see if I can put a smile on Joanie's face."

"You should know by now Jamie, that there's only one thing can do the job!"

Lyn laughed at Denise as the bass player performed a couple of vulgar pelvic thrusts in Caroline's direction.

"Ok. I'll do it. I'll shut my eyes and pretend she's Mia Farrow."

It was gone three o'clock and the owls were hooting in the trees as Lyn, tired but happy, turned the Jag onto the driveway. As she opened the front door she could hear the answerphone bleeping in the hallway. Walking over to the phone she could see there was one message alert. Pressing the 'play' button she was dismayed to hear the familiar voice of her ex-husband.

'Hi Lyn, I've been trying to call you on your mobile, but there's no answer. Where are you? We need to talk. Call me back.'

She had put her mobile on silent during the gig, and had forgotten all about it. On checking she found there had been three missed calls from Neil. She shrugged her shoulders and went upstairs to bed.

CHAPTER 28

THE TELEPHONE'S SHRILL tone sounded as though it was coming from a long way off. Waking up with a jolt, she reached out a hand from under the sheet and kept her eyes closed, whilst fumbling about on top of the bedside cabinet until she located the receiver.

"Hmmm?" Her mouth was as dry as the bottom of a parrot's cage.

"Are you still in bed? It's eleven thirty!"

"Neil; what do you want?" More awake now she sat up and took a sip from a bottle of water. It tasted like nectar.

"When have you ever still been in bed at eleven thirty on a Sunday morning?"

"I had a late night." She yawned and shook her head.

"Anyone I know?"

"None of your business. Can we get to the point please?"

"Janice's husband has filed for divorce. He wants half the house."

"So? What's that got to do with me?"

"Their house is on the market. If they get a buyer we're going to need somewhere else to live."

"I can't see where I fit into all this."

"We want to move into the house in Epsom."

With the implications of his few short words, a rage started to well up from deep inside her at the sudden collapse of all her carefully thought out plans, the loss of her future income, and the fact that her ex-husband had the cheek to want to live in *her* beautiful house with his new mistress.

"No way! When the tenants' contract finishes at the end of next month, it's going on the market. Both our names are on the deeds, and when it's sold we'll take half each and that'll be an end to it. Miss Pinky Pants and you will have to look elsewhere!"

Wide awake now and fuming, she threw back the sheet and used her shoulder to hold the phone up against her left ear while she tied the cord to her dressing gown around her waist.

"Cheers for that." There was a *tut* of annoyance at the other end, and then all she heard was a click and then the dialling tone.

Too angry to even try to go back to sleep, she went downstairs to make a cup of coffee. She sighed with the knowledge that she would have to phone the Denneys sometime that day and give them the news that their contract was not going to be renewed.

She wanted to hit something in frustration. *She had just got some semblance of a life back together, and now the bastard was knocking her down again!* She slammed her coffee cup down on the kitchen table a little too vigorously, spilling some of its contents onto the tablecloth. A hot flush began and tears threatened at the back of her eyes, but she was determined not to cry. She finished up the rest of the coffee in the cup, and decided to have a shower and a walk along the beach to cool down, clear her head, and think.

The families had already congregated on the sands by the time she strode out, and the sun was high in the sky. Side-stepping paddling children she took off her sandals and walked barefoot along the shoreline, enjoying the feel of the cool wet sand in-between her toes. Before long she found herself outside the café. She had not been back since the incident with the young man in the balaclava, but all seemed well as she opened the door and found an empty table to sit down at.

"Hi Lyn! What are you doing here on a Sunday?" Maureen smiled and came over towards her.

"Oh. Just walking about and I fancied a cup of tea and a sandwich. I sort of missed breakfast, and this is the best place I know to get something to eat."

"Angie will come over and take your order. See you as normal tomorrow?" Maureen chuckled, but looked questioningly as Lyn nodded.

"Sure thing. I'm okay."

"Great. You don't know how guilty I feel that I went home early and left you alone here."

"He'd probably been casing the joint for days and knew there was only one of us left. Don't worry about it. It's all water under the bridge now." Lyn smiled and waved a hand in greeting to a young girl approaching with a pencil and notebook.

"Hello Angie. I'm Lyn; I work here during the week. I don't think we've met before."

"Hi Lyn. I've heard a lot about you, especially recently with the police visit and all. You must be very brave."

The girl had a local accent, and Lyn enjoyed the refreshing sound of a Cornish dialect triumphing over the voices of an execrable family of Brummies at the next table.

"Not really. I was terrified, but thankfully all ended well." "What can I get you?"

"Prawn mayo sandwich on brown bread and a cup of tea please."

It seemed strange sitting at the table and being served instead of working in the kitchen. Lyn looked through the window at the beach as she ate, not thinking of anything at all in particular, and when there was a lull Maureen joined her at the table.

"Your boyfriend was in here yesterday asking about you." She giggled as Lyn rolled her eyes to the heavens.

"Oh no, not again!"

"He seems a perfect poppet and he's very keen, bless him."

"I knew I hadn't heard the last of that one."

Lyn laughed as Maureen pulled up a chair.

"This is my last season you know; I'm selling up and retiring at the end of October." Maureen automatically collected Lyn's empty plate and put it on a tray.

"Really? I didn't know you were thinking of retiring; you don't look old enough." She had thought her boss was of a similar age to herself.

"It's time to go; I'm finding it tiring now, and I'm looking forward to putting my feet up and having a bit of a rest."

"What will happen to the café then?"

"I'll sell it as a going concern. It's a little goldmine in the summer, as you know."

"How much will you be asking for it?"

A plan had begun to form in her head. Perhaps Neil's bombshell could be turned around to her advantage after all. She would go home and give it some thought.

She looked around as she left the café in case Peter Davies was skulking behind the sea wall, but fortunately he was nowhere to be seen. However, on returning home and checking her MatchULike inbox, there was one unread message.

Dear Lyn, I am just wondering how you are after that nasty incident.

Sincerely,

Peter Davies'

He had bought her dinner and looked after her when she was distressed. He deserved some sort of answer. Scratching her head she came up with a reply.

Dear Peter, I am fine now. Thanks for everything you did for me.

Regards,

Lyn'

The reply was almost instantaneous.

Dear Lyn, I am a Governor of the Trelawny Grove secondary school. The local amateur dramatic group are putting on a production of 'The Gondoliers' next Friday night at the school, and I have a spare ticket. Would you like it? The concert starts at 19:00hrs sharp.

Sincerely,

Peter'

She loved Gilbert's witty lyrics and Sullivan's music. She had been to many G&S concerts, but never 'The Gondoliers.' She had a satnav and could meet him at the school. It would be a night out, and he did not need to find out where she lived at all.

'*Dear Peter, all I need is the postcode and I can meet you there.*'
Lyn'

CHAPTER 29

THE BUILDING HAD an unused air to it that she remembered feeling at the start of each school term. The floors were polished to perfection in readiness to be scuffed into submission by hundreds of pairs of new shoes. Lyn stood by the entrance to the hall and waved to a now familiar silver-haired figure dressed impeccably in a dove grey three piece suit, white shirt, and dark grey tie, standing by the stage and talking to a rather overweight elderly lady holding a violin. On seeing her he made his way towards the entrance, a piece of paper in his hand.

"Hello Lyn! I have your ticket here."

"Thanks. I must say I've never seen a production of 'The Gondoliers". Lyn took the ticket and smiled.

"Pick a seat. I can meet up with you at the interval, but I'll be conducting the orchestra for the evening."

"Really? I wouldn't have taken you for the musical sort." She felt some relief at being able to enjoy the concert in peace without having to make conversation with him.

"It's a hobby now, but I used to play the trumpet in the regiment's brass band on a number of ceremonial occasions, and later on in life taught theory at the corps' music school."

"Thank you for inviting me."

"Not at all, but it's nearly 18:50 hours; time to muster the troops."

Lyn tried not to giggle as Peter gave a stiff bow in her direction and took his place on the podium, to be followed in by members of the cast and orchestra. When he lifted his baton at precisely seven o'clock to begin the overture, Lyn was surprised at the level of competence and quite professional performance of the players. She found she was enjoying the concert immensely, and to make some conversation decided to mention the fact in the interval.

"You're running a tight ship here, Peter. The standard is excellent. It's just occurred to me that you must be the one in charge of the orchestra and putting this concert all together."

"As I said, a little hobby of mine."

"There's obviously more to you than meets the eye. You're a modest man, Peter Davies."

"I also have many spare tickets. There isn't a Mrs Davies; in fact there never was. I'm not a widower, as I said online. I gave my life to the Army, and am rather overwhelmed around the female sex as I never actually married. Each member of the cast gets four tickets for family and friends, but Lyn, you are the first person who has ever agreed to take one of my tickets and attend a concert."

"I am honoured, Peter. Any time you have a concert on, just let me know."

"We're rehearsing Carmina Burana; should be ready for the Orff as they say by about the middle of November time."

"If I can I'll be there. Things will be happening in my life this autumn though, and I may have to disappear to Surrey for the odd weekend."

"What things? May I be so bold as to ask?"

"Oh, it's to do with my ex-husband and our house."

"Ah, I see. Best to keep mum then."

"Probably, but I know I'll be able to use up at least another one of your tickets besides mine."

"Your boyfriend?"

"Well, Jamie is a friend, but not my boyfriend. Actually she's a girl, but I know she would love to come along to something like this."

She stifled another giggle as Peter gave her an odd look and straightened up a bit taller.

"Ah. One who bats for the Middlesex regiment then?"

"Not at all. Jamie is a man in a girl's body." "I see."

In order to stop her mouth from turning up at the corners, Lyn turned away to place her drink down on a nearby table. She was not sure if Peter was quite *au fait* with the complexities of human sexuality.

CHAPTER 30

THE DENNEYS HAD left the house spick and span. The usual decaying blanket of autumn leaves had been swept up from the patio, and even the rusting barbeque looked as if it had had a makeover. Lyn heard Neil's van pull up on the driveway, and opened the front door. She sighed with relief when she saw he was alone, but noticed he was unsmiling as he opened the car door.

"Alright?"

She heard his familiar voice and for a split second it was as though things were as they used to be, and she was standing on their doorstep welcoming him home from a trip away. *A trip that he'd made to see his mistress?*

"Yes I'm fine. How are you?"

"I'm going to be a father next May."

"Congratulations. Now we know whose fault it was that we never had children." She felt a stab of jealousy at the mental image of him sitting down reading stories to his child, with the inevitable Miss Pinky Pants simpering in the background.

"Janice wanted to have a baby before she gets too old. She's thirty five now."

"Really? As old as that? I suppose she'd better get a move on then." She wanted to slap him, and mentally counted to ten before exhaling slowly.

"Another saucer of milk darling? It'll help the fur-ball you've swallowed."

"Look, I haven't come here to argue. The completion date is next Friday and we need to make sure the house is empty for the new owners. I'll take the curtains that I can use, if you'd like to check in the loft."

"Yeah. I'll get my ladder from the van and have a look."

She hated the house now with a vengeance. All the years she had spent dusting, polishing, cleaning, and trying to conceive seemed a total waste of her life. Her footsteps echoed on the bare floorboards as she trudged from room to room trying to block out the memories.

"There's nothing left up in the loft. Which curtains do you want taking down?" Neil appeared in their bedroom doorway holding a ladder under one arm.

"I've changed my mind. Leave them all here unless you want them." Lyn pushed past Neil to get out of the bedroom, as the ghosts of their breathless and entwined bodies were just too much for her to cope with.

"Janice has a different colour scheme in mind I think. Let the new owners have them." He turned towards her on the landing. "Will you be okay for money?"

"Fine. I'm going to buy the beach café that I've been working in this summer with my half of the proceeds. It's a good investment and it'll give me an income for as long as I want to work. The owner is retiring, and I'm looking forward to being self-employed. At least I'll know how to do the tax returns." She gave him a faint smile and enjoyed his brief look of complete surprise.

"Well. I hope it works out for you."

"I'm sure it will. I've got enough money to live on for the winter, and I'll make damn sure to give it my best shot." She suddenly felt empowered, free, and at nobody's mercy.

"Well, good luck; I'll take the keys if you like and drop them off at the estate agent, if you want to get back home before it gets too late." He held out his hand for her key.

"Thanks." She saw his oh-so-familiar fingers reach out with the permanent ingrained dirt on them of a man who works with his hands. She remembered how they had caressed her breasts, her hair, and her body; how they had held her tight that last time while she had sobbed the bitter tears of childlessness, certain in the knowledge that they were too old to adopt. She suddenly wanted to run to the safety of his arms, and let him stroke her hair and assure her that everything was going to be alright.

She put her key in his hand:

"Cheers. See ya, Lyn."

"Bye Neil." She held her head high, stopped her tears in their tracks, and with flaming cheeks walked with as much dignity as she could muster down the stairs, through the front door, and out to her waiting car.

CHAPTER 31

"IT'S MY BELIEF that you need cheering up. I've had some good news, so I'm going to have a coming out party."

Lyn wanted so much to shake herself out of the pit of depression she had fallen into after realising with a growing certainty that she was now definitely on her own. The big house in Epsom had gone, and with that her comfortable income. Neil had fallen headfirst into the welcoming arms of Janice, enveloping him finally into the family life Lyn had tried so hard to attain, and five months of winter beckoned before she could take over from Maureen and start to try and make a living from the café.

"What are you on about?" She sighed with irritation as she placed plates and cutlery into the dishwasher and flicked the switch.

"I've had a letter from my consultant. I'm going to get a dick!"

"Oh, that's wonderful Jamie!" She felt guilty at being so bad-tempered, and was genuinely pleased for her friend.

"A real one! I'll be able to stand at the urinals in the men's instead of going in the cubicle. It definitely calls for a coming out party don't you think?"

"What's coming out? Not the dick I hope; you'll frighten the horses!" Lyn giggled and felt glad Jamie had invited herself round for lunch. She had started to feel better already.

"Well, I'll be so proud of it that I'll want to wave it about for everyone to see, but no, it'll be a coming-out-as-a-man party. I'll invite you, the girls from the band, Ed and his bird, and some mates from the pub. I'm going to get as pissed as a newt."

"Good for you; I think I'll be joining you. When's it going to be then?"

"Looks like it's scheduled for two weeks' time; the twenty third of November."

"The dick or the party?"

"The party of course! The dick's getting done on the fifteenth."

"I'm definitely free on the twenty third. On the fifteenth I'm going to one of

Peter Davies' concerts. You could have come as well, but I guess you'll be er….otherwise engaged."

"Yeah, too right. Are you going out with him now then?" Jamie looked slightly aghast.

"No! Not in that way." Lyn rolled her eyes to the heavens and smiled: "He conducts his local Am-Dram orchestra. He's given concert tickets, but only has me to give them to. It's a bit sad really. He's got nobody; a bit like me, but worse I think."

"I'm not surprised if he goes around stalking people."

"I think he's just a little strange because he's been in the Forces and hasn't been used to being around women. He seems a perfect gent really."

"Hasn't he tried anything yet then?"

"Not at all. It's quite lovely! After the last concert he walked me to my car, said goodnight, and then I drove home."

"Watch out. He's probably storing it up for next time. Do the chastity belt up a notch."

"He's harmless. He was a godsend that night at the café."

"Only because he was stalking you in the first place."

"I think you're wrong."

"I'll bet my new dick that he's the biggest perv going." "I don't want your dick!" Lyn threw back her head and laughed.

"I'll give it to you on a plate if I'm wrong, and believe me, I'm not wrong!"

"Well, he can't stalk me anymore. The café's closed for the winter, and he doesn't know where I live. He has to wait until he sees me at his concerts." An element of doubt started to creep into her mind that perhaps Jamie could be telling the truth.

"Just don't tell him anything. I've got a feeling about that prick."

"You're wrong; you're so wrong."

"Well, as I said; you can have my new dick on a plate if I am."

CHAPTER 32

"FANCY STRADDLING THE VFR tonight? I'm all for it instead of going out with pervy Pete" Lyn plonked a bunch of grapes down by Jamie's side on the hospital bed.

"Er.... don't think I'll be straddling anything for a while, but thanks for the grapes." Jamie smiled weakly, "I can't eat anything yet. I'm still throwing up after the anaesthetic."

"You'll be fine. I've just popped in to make sure you're back with us."

"Yeah, give me a few days and I'll be raring to go."

"When are you coming home?"

"In a couple of days I think. Just got to make sure everything's working ok."

"Is it?"

"Don't know yet. I haven't long woken up."

"I'll come in tomorrow and let you know how it went with pervy Pete."

"If you're still alive."

"If you don't shut up about him I'll tell the nurses your religious beliefs state that you need a circumcision."

"Will you bugger off?" Jamie leaned back, his face as white as the pillow case.

"I'm going. I'll let you rest now, but I'll be back tomorrow. Sleep well." She smiled at her friend and stood up to go.

"Sorry I'm not very chatty. Pass me that sick bowl before you go."

The floor polish was doing its best to recover from the last few weeks of the school term, and the corridors smelt of stale cabbage and sweaty socks. Lyn made her way to the main hall, mindful of Jamie's advice.

"Good evening Lyn; are you ready to enjoy some debauchery and drunken student songs tonight then?"

"Eh?" She glanced quizzically at Peter and wondered if Jamie had been right all along.

"Carmina Burana. It's a good thing the choir will be singing in German and Latin, that's all I can say."

"Oh. Well, my German is non-existent, and I only know *illegitmus non tatum carborundum* in Latin." She gave a nervous laugh.

"My prowess in both languages is *non gradus anus rodentum,* but I hope you will enjoy the music anyway."

She liked the quaint way in which he gave a slight bow to her before walking away to the conductor's podium. She looked through the packed programme he had put in her hand, and realised the concert would not be ending until quite late. She decided to find a seat near the door in case the music was not to her taste, thus enabling her to make an unobtrusive getaway.

"Are we ready for the Orff?"

Lyn heard some members of the orchestra tittering politely as Peter raised his baton. However, she was unprepared for the wall of sound and the shivers down her spine that hit her as *O Fortuna* began. As she listened she vaguely remembered hearing the tune years before on TV in an advert for aftershave; a man, presumably as odoriferous as a cage of old mice, surfed giant waves as *O Fortuna* played in the background. As the concert progressed she totally forgot about making a hasty exit, and was in awe of the amount of time and effort that Peter had obviously put in to preparing the choir and orchestra. At the interval she was the first to make her way to the refreshments table to congratulate him.

"Peter, this concert is spectacular; worthy of any professional show."

"Thank you." She noticed the little bow again. "It's a hobby of mine. Not much else to fill my days now I'm retired."

"I wasn't sure it would be to my taste, but I take it all back." She smiled as she sipped an ice-cold cola.

"I prefer the second half. Keep half an ear cocked for *Veni Venias and Blanziflor et Helena.*"

"I will."

When *O Fortuna* sounded again for the final time, Lyn realised she had thoroughly enjoyed the evening. She waited until the crowd around Peter had dispersed, and then went up to him.

"I'm off now, but just wanted to congratulate you on a wonderful show."

"Glad you enjoyed it. I'll walk you to your car, and then I'll help clear up in here."

She would have rather gone to her car alone, but could hardly turn down his offer. However, on arrival back at the car park she stared with dismay at the Jag's flat rear tyre.

"I knew I should have got round to joining the AA. Neil always took care of the car." She sighed with frustration, knowing she did not possess the physical strength or the knowledge needed to change a wheel.

"I'll run you home after I've finished clearing up in the hall, and then I'll change the tyre for you tomorrow when I've collected some tools together and put my old jeans on. The car will be fine here overnight."

"Thanks so much. I'll come back in then and help you put the chairs away."

All the while she had kept her address secret, but now he would find out where she lived. She could hear Jamie's voice in her head sending out multiple warnings, but at 11 o'clock on a cold November night all she wanted to do was to get home again.

"Where do you live, my dear?"

"Prospect Road, Hayle. You can drop me off at the end of my road to save you having to turn round. It's a narrow street."

"No, no; at this time of night I shall make sure I see you right to the door."

Shit! Lyn sighed and fastened her seat belt.

He drove at an irritatingly slow speed. She was tired and annoyed with herself for having failed to register with the AA.

"I'll call a mechanic out tomorrow. You don't have to put yourself out."

"It's no trouble. We can have lunch somewhere afterwards if you like."

"I'll let you know. I shall be visiting a friend in hospital, and I think visiting hours might coincide with that." She felt desperate to get away from his clutches. "Where are you going? That's not the way to Hayle." Her heart began to pound in her chest, and she mentally kicked herself for being so stupid as to get in his car.

"This is a quicker way. It cuts about 15 minutes off the journey. Are you okay? You seem somewhat agitated."

"No, no; I'm fine. I'm fine."

She did not recognise where she was at all, but when he drove into Hayle's main shopping area she realised he had been telling the truth all along.

"You're right, Peter. I didn't know about this short cut."

"You learn something every day. Mission accomplished. Damsel in distress safely delivered to Prospect Road. Which number?"

"It's called Rose Cottage. The one on the left up there with the trellis over the front door."

"Very nice too." He pulled up and leaned over her to open the passenger door, causing Lyn to give an involuntary flinch backwards. She felt foolish when he smiled at her.

"You don't have to worry about me, my dear. I've had a 'gentleman's operation' for cancer. I don't have the wherewithal to carry out any..... *ahem*....procedures, and after the oestrogen treatment, have no inclination to do so anyway. You are completely safe. As I said on the computer, I'm just looking for companionship."

Her laugh echoed down the quiet road.

"Peter…. I look forward to lunch out tomorrow. Also I could do with some of your oestrogen if you don't mind!" Her relief was almost tangible.

"What about your friend in hospital?" His face remained deadpan.

"He's had a 'gentleman's operation' as well. I'll visit him in the evening instead."

"There's a lot of it about."

CHAPTER 33

"THE LUNCH IS on me today as thanks for putting on my spare wheel. No

arguments":

Lyn waved in the waiter's direction for the bill, while watching Peter putting two lumps of brown sugar in his coffee and stirring it loudly with a spoon.

"Well, I thank you most sincerely for a pleasant lunch with equally pleasant company my dear. Excuse my casual attire though."

"Peter, you don't have to worry about a thing. You're a perfect gentleman whatever you're wearing. When's the next concert?"

"Christmastime. We'll be rehearsing carols and suchlike during December."

The depressing thought suddenly came to her that this year she had nobody to spend Christmas Day with. She remembered all the years when she and Neil had gone to some fancy restaurant for Christmas Day, had eaten too much and drank too much, and had then collapsed in each other's arms all afternoon, too full to move. Christmas was a time for families, and now she had none. This year she would be cooking for one and eating alone.

"Are you alright my dear? You look a little down."

"I'm okay. Where do you go on Christmas Day?"

"I have a tiresome older brother and cretinous sister-in-law. Exactly a month before the big day I will receive a phone call as he carries out his once-a-year sibling duty and invites me for lunch. I usually manage to escape by about 5 o'clock though, back to the comfort of base camp."

"You're lucky to even have a brother." Lyn chuckled. "Now I'm divorced I have nobody; I'd even welcome a tiresome brother if I had one."

"Then you must share mine. Why should I have all the aggravation? William was Mother's favourite, you know. I was bundled off into the Army, and he took over the farm. Daphne doesn't know her arse from her elbow, although she cooks a passable Christmas dinner."

"They sound divine. I'll certainly keep it in mind. Thank you." She liked it when a chink of humour fought its way past his defences.

"Your friend whom you're visiting in hospital later on; is he not your partner then?"

"He's just a friend. I have nobody special now, Peter."

"Then it's their loss. I would be happy to be your companion, if you so wish."

"For the winter months I think I might take you up on that. From April until the end of October I've taken over at the beach café, so I'll be busy stocking up at the wholesalers, interviewing staff, and running around between the tables and so on. I think I'll have plenty to do then."

"I'm thinking I'll be coming along every day for my elevenses." He smiled and drained his cup.

"You only get free coffee if you clear the tables."

"A pleasure my dear; a pleasure."

"Wow! You look so much better tonight!" Lyn thought Jamie looked almost back to his old self.

"Yeah, I can't wait to get out of here. I've peed and peed until I can't pee no more. The nurses are very pleased; they're obsessed with my bowels though for some reason. I'm just waiting for the quack to sign me off and then I can go. Ed's picking me up later."

"Oh no; you can't go home yet."

"Eh? Why not?"

"Pervy Pete turned out to be perfect Pete. You've got to have that circumcision now. I was right. He even changed my tyre when it was flat."

"No! Really? Well I was only joking; I knew all the time he was a good'un.

Bring him to my party!"

Lyn laughed at the sight of Jamie holding a hand over his new nether regions as if to guard them.

"Well, I'm not sure if it'll be his thing. He's a bit old fashioned."

"Nah. Anything goes at my party. He'll fit right in."

The Cod Father' had a 'closed' sign in the window as Lyn drove

past the shop and parked the car. Music blared out from the open front door of Jamie's house and into the street outside. She saw Peter looking out of the passenger window nervously as he recognised the surroundings.

"Will that chap who works in the fish and chip shop be at the party? I don't think it's a good idea that I go with you after all, my dear."

"Everything's fine Peter. It was just a misunderstanding." Lyn smiled at him as she turned off the engine.

They followed Alice Cooper's voice down the hallway and into Jamie's front room. Cat leapt from her chair to kiss Lyn on both cheeks.

"Lyn! How are you?"

"I'm fine. How are you? Any more gigs?"

"Jamie's got us a gig at the pub next door on Friday week. Coming?"

"Sure. Cat, this is a friend, Peter."

"No man's ever bowed to me before, Peter!"

"My pleasure."

"Pete! Sorry we got off on the wrong foot last time. Hello Lyn!" Jamie bounded over to them, and Lyn found herself enveloped in a bear hug.

"I see you're back to normal then." She laughed at Jamie's exuberance.

"The op went well. Jamie's back and rocking."

"Ah, yes; it took me a couple of weeks to recover after I had mine done five years' ago, but thankfully I've never needed to wear a bra on the hormone treatment." Peter gave a little chuckle

"You've had the op too? Jamie looked at Peter with a surprised look on his face.

"Jamie……." Lyn tried to interrupt.

"Yes. I worried about growing breasts, but thankfully all is well."

"You should have seen the size of mine; I had to have them cut off in the end."

"Good God!"

"Yeah; size 42GG. Bloody things; I couldn't find a bra that fitted."

"Oh, my goodness! You were unlucky! Perhaps you were on too high a dose of oestrogen?" Peter looked down at his chest as if to check for unwelcome bulges.

"Oestrogen? Nah! You shouldn't be on oestrogen! What sort of a fucking doctor have you got? He ought to be struck off!" Jamie looked aghast.

"Jamie……" Lyn tried again to interrupt.

"All well down below Pete?" Jamie looked puzzled, sipped a pint of beer with one hand, and pointed to his crotch with the other.

"'Things,' as it transpired, were never really quite the same again I'm afraid. All I can say is that it's a good thing I never married."

"Sorry to hear that, but I've got no trouble with *my* prosthesis."

"Prosthesis?"

"Yeah. You know; the rod on my rod, so to speak. I can't wait to put it into practise. Know what I mean?" Jamie gave a leer and a pelvic thrust in Peter's direction.

"Jamie, Peter's had a different kind of operation; it wasn't the same as yours." Lyn was grateful to be able to get a word in edgeways. The two men looked

at each other in relief, before Jamie burst out laughing and clapped Peter on the back.

"Come on Lyn; leave the men to it for a minute. Caroline wants everyone to meet her new girlfriend."

The room was hot and crowded with people she mostly did not recognise. Lyn followed Cat to where Caroline, alias Joan Bonk'em, sat in one corner on somebody's lap.

"Put her down Reggie; you don't know where she's been. Reggie this is Lyn; a friend of ours. Lyn, meet Regina, Caroline's current."

"Hi Lyn. Sorry if I was a pain in the arse last time we met." Caroline kissed the forehead of somebody Lyn could not see, and then she saw a face appear around the side of Caroline's dark curtain of hair:

"Hi Lyn; I'm Reggie."

Lyn reached over to shake Reggie's extended hand. She noticed a mass of blonde dreadlocks and startling pair of pale grey eyes.

"Pleased to meet you Reggie. Caroline, you weren't a pain in the arse last time at all."

"Thank fuck for that."

Lyn looked back at Peter, who stood ill-at-ease amongst Jamie's odd- looking cluster of cohorts:

"I'll better get back to my friend."

"Ooh….have you got a new boyfriend then?"   Caroline gave Peter the once-over."

"He's just a friend, but feeling a little bit out of it I think."

"Go upstairs and give him one. That'll sort him out. They're queuing up outside the bedroom." Caroline and Reggie giggled together.

"If only the solution could be that simple." Lyn forced a wide smile to cover the fact that she felt at least a hundred and fifty years old.

CHAPTER 34

"JUST CHECKING UP to see if you're still alive." Lyn let her imagination run riot as to Jamie's possible appearance on the morning after the night before.

"What a party, eh? Did you see Caroline's new bird? I saw you dancing with her at one point. I could definitely go for that one." A large yawn emanated from Jamie's mobile phone.

"You'd need to go back to your original gender then; she likes the girls I'm afraid."

"Shit. How's pervy Peter?"

"Not a peep out of him all night. He's still asleep in my spare room."

"What! Did you lock your bedroom door?"

"Don't have any locks. He's harmless; I told you before. It was late; he'd left his car at mine, but I think someone must have given him doubles instead of singles. There was no way he was driving home."

"Ah; that was probably Ed. I remember the bet was on to see who could loosen old Pete up a bit."

"He's alright. I hope Ed hasn't killed him; I'm not sure he's used to drinking that much."

"Open the door and have a look."

"I couldn't. He might be stark naked. Oh; my landline's ringing Jamie; thanks for a lovely party."

"I'm back at work on Wednesday, but will see you at the Zepp gig."

"Okay; bye."

By the time she managed to get to the phone it had stopped ringing, but she then heard Peter calling from the upstairs landing.

"I answered the phone as I didn't know where you were. There's a gentleman on the line for you."

"Thanks Peter!" She picked up the phone and heard him replace the receiver in the spare bedroom before turning the hot water switch on for a shower in the en-suite:

"Who's that prat that answered the phone?"

"Oh. Hello Neil. To what do I owe the pleasure?"

"Is he your boyfriend?"

"Yes, but what's it got to do with you?"

"Has he been there all night? Are you having sex with him?"

"He lives here now. We're at it night and day." She wanted to wound him with words, just as he had inadvertently slain her on mentioning his impending fatherhood.

"Well, it didn't take you long to get back in the saddle did it?"

"No it didn't; I found somebody kind, and who wanted to be with me. What do you want?" She was enjoying herself. The lies came easily; one after the other.

"Nothing. I was just checking you're okay. It seems I'm wasting my time though."

"Thanks for calling, but I'm fine."

"I'm always here if you're ever in trouble. We were married too long for me to forget you completely."

"You're a prince of the highest order."

"Sorry for being such a total bastard."

"You can't help it. You're a man."

"Is the coast clear? Didn't want to interrupt your phone call."

Lyn smiled at Peter, slightly pale, but freshly shaven, showered, and neatly dressed.

"There's nothing to interrupt; just my twat of an ex-husband ringing up. For a moment I was worried that he was after this house as well."

"Was he?"

"No. It seems Cornwall is going to be my home now."

"That's AOK as far as I'm concerned." "Coffee and a bacon sandwich?"

"Ah; just coffee please. The old alimentary canal is a bit out of sorts this morning."

"That was all the double vodkas. I think Ed got a bit carried away."

"I haven't felt like this since the day after my passing out parade. I think I actually did pass out so I'm told, but the whole incident is now thankfully just a blur."

"One coffee coming up." She smiled as she switched on the kettle.

"Thinking about it, I'm going home now. Must stay close to base today; feel a little delicate, and don't want to show myself up any further."

She switched off the kettle and tried not to laugh as Peter, slightly green about the gills, quickly gathered his belongings and put on his jacket.

"I shall bid you farewell for the time being, but will be in touch when I have totally recovered from this minor setback."

"As you wish, Peter. As you wish." She chuckled as she closed the door behind him.

The hours stretched out before her, and the rain ran down the windows in rivulets. Having nothing pressing to do, nowhere to go and nobody to see, she decided to ease her thumping head and return to bed for the duration of the morning.

CHAPTER 35

AS THE DAYS shortened, the golden sands lost their allure, and one by one the holiday cottages and second homes emptied. Mid-December brought the usual snow, wind, and hail; the sea rose and fell angrily in icy grey waves, and a walk along the empty beach was an endurance test and gave her no joy. The band's gigs were few and far between, and Jamie seemed to be enthralled with Sara, his MatchULike Mia Farrow, and the current love of his life. Peter's time was taken up rehearsing with the Am-Dram orchestra and choir for their Christmas show, and Lyn was at a loose end, yearning for the start of Spring and the chance to work again at her new project. She invested prematurely in some brushes and several pots of magnolia paint, ready for giving the café a face lift at the start of the season. Most days saw her walking past the boarded up windows, checking that the front door was still locked and bolted securely.

Messages had stopped arriving in her MatchULike inbox, and she could see no new profiles that appealed. As the days progressed through December she realised with dismay that she was going to have to endure her first Christmas alone. She was tempted to take up Peter's offer, but did not really want to intrude on the once-a-year family visit with his brother. She knew she would feel in the way, and wondered if Peter's brother really wanted a stranger in the house on Christmas Day.

She had her hair highlighted specially, and dressed smartly on the night of the Am-Dram Christmas concert. She felt depressed and hoped her new outfit was going to lift her spirits out of the doldrums. She sighed as she gave in her ticket at the entrance to the school hall, and stood alone at the back looking around for Peter.

"Lyn! Lovely to see you! I'm so sorry I've not been in touch lately. As you can see, I've been rather busy. You look delightful by the way."

She smiled at Peter as he bounded towards her, full of energy and enthusiasm.

"Thanks. I think I need something like this to keep me busy for the winter months. I'm at a bit of a loose end." She felt like crying with loneliness, and yearned for even the briefest of hugs from another human being.

"I meant to call you; Daphne wants to know if you're a vegetarian or not, but I warn you now that her past nut roasts have clogged up manoeuvres for a week."

"Why is Daphne asking?" She could not help but emit a giggle.

"Christmas Day of course. She doesn't want to give you a turkey leg and send you screaming from the room."

"Oh, I don't like to intrude on your family on Christmas Day, Peter."

"It's no intrusion. It'll be lovely to have your company. I remembered you had vegetarian fare when we dined previously, so I thought that maybe turkey was off?"

"No, no I love turkey. Are you sure you want me to come?" She suddenly felt her spirits rise in a positively upward direction.

"Daphne has never been so excited. I think she's even constructed a new pudding for the occasion. William tells me it's a sort of bomb shape. Now excuse me, but duty calls." He gave a small salute and turned on his heel towards the orchestra pit.

She felt inordinately happy for the rest of the evening, and sang along lustily with the choruses. The thought of not being alone on the most family-orientated day of the year was enough to put the roses back in her cheeks and a smile on her face.

"William and Daphne; may I present my good friend Lyn?"

"I've been looking forward to meeting you since Peter first mentioned he was bringing someone. Come in and make yourself at home!" Daphne bubbled and sparkled, and Lyn felt genuine warmth emanating from the plump and homely-looking middle-aged woman.

"Hello Lyn; it's been at least forty years since Peter has brought anybody to our table. We're honoured to have you as our guest."

Lyn looked at a slightly older version of Peter and wondered how their mother could have had the patience to imbue two small boys with such impeccable manners.

"Thank you. It's lovely to meet you both. I've brought some small gifts as a thank you." She held out two presents wrapped in tissue paper.

"This is a first; Peter never brings us gifts! What'll you have to drink? We have most things in stock: Wine; sherry; gin; you name it and we've probably got it."

"Peter's driving, so make it a gin and tonic please." She enjoyed the attention of William helping her off with her coat. She felt like a princess.

"Lunch won't be long, and in case you don't like Christmas pudding I've made another dessert." Daphne smiled and smoothed down her hair.

"Sounds lovely. Can I do anything to help?"

"No, just sit yourself down and relax." Daphne disappeared into the kitchen, leaving Lyn with William and Peter, who seemed in no hurry to catch up after a year apart.

Sipping her drink and eager to break the silence, she looked out of the window at the acres of arable fields stretching out far into the distance.

"It's a beautiful farm. Is all the land yours that I can see?" She looked quizzically at William, who nodded.

"Yes; well, father inherited the farm originally, but I took it over when he passed away. I'm retired now, and our son farms the land. He and his wife live in that cottage across the yard, but they're off visiting her folks today."

"I expect your mother was a remarkable woman too; running the farm and bringing you and Peter up."

She noticed an almost imperceptible knowing look travelling between the two brothers. Peter remained silent, but William soon recovered his composure.

"Er…..mother was erudite; very learned, witty, and accomplished musically, but alas not cut out to be your typical farmer's wife."

Lyn thought it best not to pursue the subject. With some relief she heard Daphne calling them to the table, which to her delight was fairly groaning under the weight of traditional home-made Christmas fare.

"Daphne; you're a marvel to have to have made all this yourself!" Lyn was impressed, causing Daphne to beam from ear to ear.

"I love Christmastime. There's nothing better than a day's baking, and seeing the family enjoying what I've prepared. "

"Wow. You're just what I would expect a farmer's wife to be like!" Lyn chuckled and took her place at the table.

"Peter; you always carve on Christmas Day. I like to sit and be waited on." William smiled at his younger brother.

"I haven't done this since last Christmas, so the first few slices may go slightly awry." Peter stood up stiffly, took up the carving knife and fork, and bent his willowy frame over the roasted turkey. "Hold out your plates please; Lyn, you can be the first."

While Peter was heaping her plate with meat, Lyn looked over his shoulder towards a canvas portrait of a beautiful, smiling red-haired young girl of about or 15 that was hanging in a gilt frame upon the wall.

"Who's that girl...if I may be so nosy as to ask?" She pointed a finger towards the picture.

"That's our elder sister Amelia; the only picture we have of her I'm afraid." William looked towards the portrait and then back at his brother, who continued carving in silence.

"You never mentioned that you had a sister, Peter." Lyn took her plate away and passed Daphne's plate to him.

"She died soon after she sat for that portrait. Accidental death at boarding school." Peter looked wistfully at the picture for a moment, and then continued carving the turkey.

CHAPTER 36

"WELL, I CAN'T say when I enjoyed a meal more. Lovely food and delightful company. I'm so glad I was invited today." Lyn placed a pile of dirty plates next to the sink, and picked up a tea towel. "I'm definitely going to dry up for you. You've worked so hard today Daphne."

"That's so kind of you. We'll let the men talk then, while we wash up and have a natter." Daphne filled the large enamel sink with soap suds.

Lyn felt her heart suddenly start to race and the beginning of another hot flush. She fanned her face with her hand and rolled her eyes at Daphne.

"It's terrible this menopause malarkey isn't it?" She sighed as she looked at the older woman.

"I'm still getting the odd flush fifteen years' later."

"Good God!"

"Sorry if that's not the answer you wanted." Daphne smiled as she rinsed the plates.

"It's okay. I'm getting used to them now." She had another thought. "Do they get on well, William and Peter?" With curiosity, Lyn had noticed the brothers' long silences.

"They never used to, but they've mellowed as they've got older. I think William would like to see his brother a bit more often, but Peter never gets in touch."

"He's said before that William was always their mother's favourite. Perhaps that was the cause of the animosity?" Lyn put a pile of clean plates back on the dresser.

"Funnily enough William has always said it was Amelia who was the favourite. Of course I never knew Edith when Amelia was alive, but apparently she was never cut out to be a farmer's wife and always complained that she had married beneath her. After Amelia died Edith went to pieces, started to resent the boys, and Peter in particular had a bit of a rough time of it."

"Oh? In what way?"

"William has sometimes said in the past that Peter was a bit of a handful as a boy; often beaten by Edith and kept in isolation. I think he must have jumped ship at the first chance he had and joined the Army. Mind you, he's had a good career, but Edith had always let Peter know he would never inherit the farm, so I suppose he had to make a go of it elsewhere."

"Poor Peter. No wonder he never married. His mother must have put him off women for life."

"He's always been shy around women, but there was a girl once; he brought her here for Christmas when Edith was getting on a bit. I remember her name was Nancy, and she had lovely dark curly hair. William and I were just married, and Edith lived in the cottage where our son lives now. I don't think I've ever spent a more uncomfortable Christmas than that one. Edith spent the whole time running Peter down and trying to make Nancy look stupid by asking her questions in that clever way she had. The girl couldn't get out of the door quick enough. You're the only other friend he's ever brought here."

"Wow. What about their father? Didn't he ever intervene?" Lyn suddenly felt as though she had known Daphne all her life.

"Old Tom? No; it was Edith who ruled the roost. Tom went out on his tractor in the mornings, came home in the evenings, and left everything else to Edith."

"Sorry to be so nosey, but what happened to Amelia?" Lyn wiped the kitchen table as she pushed her luck to try and find out the last piece in the jigsaw.

"Hung herself with the cord of her dressing gown on the last day of the summer term. I don't know - it's as though she didn't want to go home don't you think? She never left a note; just faded away without a word. Peter was about twelve, and William would have been about thirteen or fourteen. The family was never the same again." Daphne pulled the plug out of the sink and Lyn watched the soapy water drain away, as though taking some more of Amelia's lifeblood with it.

"Come back again; please don't leave it another year!" "Don't
    you worry Daphne; I'll be coming back soon for
more of your 'bombe surprise'. Lyn hugged the older woman with whom she had found a great empathy in such a short space of time.

"It came out alright didn't it? It was a bit touch and go as at one point I thought I'd used too much sherry."

"You can never use too much sherry, Daphne. Thanks for your phone number; I'll be inviting you and William round for Sunday lunch in the very near future."

"Wonderful!"

She watched as Peter hugged his sister-in –law and shook his brother's hand solemnly. After she had said goodbye to William and sat herself back in the passenger seat of Peter's car, she exhaled a big sigh of relief that the much-feared day was nearly over. Peter steered the car down the bumpy driveway, and then turned to her as he heard her relax.

"Enjoyed yourself?"

"Absolutely. Your brother is charm itself, and Daphne is just lovely. I'm inviting them, and you of course, for Sunday lunch in a couple of weeks' time as a thank you for having me today."

"You really don't have to do that."

"Daphne and I are firm friends now; she's looking forward to coming."

"There's more to it than meets the eye with my family, but I expect Daphne has blurted it all out; you can't shut the woman up." Peter sounded irritated as he pulled out onto the main road back to Hayle.

"Yes, I know about Amelia, but it'll go no further; it's none of my business anyway."

"I always wondered why she did it."

"You'll probably never know, but it's no excuse to keep your only brother and his wife at arm's length."

"I've always wanted to be away from it all; Amelia was always a shadow in the background. We've never talked about it much."

"Well there you are then; it's taken a stranger like me to bring it all out in the open."

"You're not a stranger, Lyn; you're my friend."

She smiled at him, and was so relaxed that as the car's engine stopped on her driveway, she opened her eyes and realised with some embarrassment that she had dropped off to sleep during the entire homeward journey.

"Thanks for a lovely day Peter, but as you can see I'm rather tired now." She gave an apologetic laugh as she opened the car door.

"No problem. Will phone you soon. Over and out." He chuckled as he closed the door again, waved to her, and backed the car out onto the road.

The answerphone was bleeping with the number '2' as she turned the key in the lock. On pressing the 'play' button she was surprised to hear a couple of familiar voices:

'Hey beautiful lady; Jamie here. The girls have a gig at the pub on New Year's Eve. Bring Pete along 'cos Ed wants to get him pissed again. Kissy kissy.'

She could not help but laugh at Jamie's irrepressible spirit. The next message however, came totally out of the blue:

'Hi; it's Neil. Just wishing you a happy Christmas. Hope you're having a great day.'

A faint smile played about her lips as she deleted the messages. *Yes; the day had gone much better than she could have ever hoped.*

CHAPTER 37

THE BAND WERE halfway through the first part of their set, and the pub was heaving. Lyn elbowed her way through the crowd and followed Peter up to the bar; waving to Jamie and Ed.

"Hi Lyn! Hey Pete, you old sly dog, you! It's my round; what're you having?"

Lyn saw the quick wink that passed between the brothers, and was glad she had relayed Jamie's message.

"Nothing that you're buying me, young man. I have a long memory. It took me two days to recover from our last rendezvous."

"Hey Lyn!"

She found herself enveloped in Jamie's usual bear hug.

"Happy New Year Jamie! How was your Christmas?"

"Blissful; we didn't get out of bed all day."

"Ah; thanks for sharing." She laughed. "Where's Sara then?"

"Outside having a smoke. Cat's asked her to keep Reggie amused; she's been trying to creep onto Joanic's lap on the drum stool."

"Rock and roll!" She lifted up the index and little finger of her right hand and laughed.

"Yeah."

They found an empty corner at the far end of the bar. Lyn thought that Peter seemed more at ease than previously; he had dressed down somewhat from his usual sartorial elegance, and she noticed well-pressed jeans, white trainers, crisply ironed stripy shirt, and lack of a tie.

"I've never seen you dressed so casually, Peter. I quite like it in fact." As she raised her glass for a toast she thought he could even pass muster at a Status Quo concert. "To friendship."

"Yes; to friendship." He cleared his throat and took a sip of wine. "My dear, I must thank you for accepting me into your world after our disastrous start. I can honestly say that at this precise moment I have never been happier. Daphne is beside herself with glee, due to your delightful entry into our lives."

She was touched by his honesty, and found her eyes misting over. She reached out, held his fingers with her own, and shouted over the noise of the band.

"This year has been hell for me, but with you and Jamie to help I've managed to build some sort of life here for myself. I just want the old year to disappear and the new one to start, so that I can get going on the café and really settle in." She smiled, disengaged her hand, and took a long swig of her Bacardi and coke.

"I have a feeling that next year is going to be a good year." Peter nodded his head in time to the music.

The girls stopped playing at midnight whilst Big Ben's chimes could be heard over the sound of a pyrotechnic orgasm emanating from the TV screen. Lyn laughed as Jamie and Sara were immediately locked in a passionate embrace.

"Happy New Year Lyn!"

She found herself swung around by Ed, and deposited with some ceremony back on her bar stool. She kissed his cheek and was immediately picked up again by Jamie.

"Happy New Year! Why don't you give pervy Pete a kiss?"

"Jamie; why don't you mind your own business?" She laughingly kissed him, but hoped Peter had not heard anything.

"Come on people; we're going to sing Auld Lang Syne. Join hands in a circle everyone!" Jamie's voice boomed over the fireworks.

For some reason Lyn always wanted to cry at midnight on New Year's Eve, and as she linked arms with Peter and Jamie she felt her throat choke up with emotion. All the badness of the previous year was being washed away, and the excitement of a new year was yet to come, but without Neil. *She had always kissed Neil on New Year's Eve, but where was he? Was he thinking about her and of old times?*

She could not stop the tears from falling. She sang and cried for the loss of her old life and the uncertainty of the new. She cried for all the babies she had never had. She cried for the sake of crying on New Year's Eve.

"My dear; permit me to give you a handkerchief. I can vouch for its pristine condition."

"Dear Peter. Thank you. I shall be alright in a moment." She wiped her eyes and focused on the finale of the firework display, while Cat tuned her guitar, eager to resume playing.

"Permit me to kiss your cheek. I find I am unable to resist the urge."

"If you kiss me I may have to return the favour." She laughed through her tears as she walked into Peter's open arms, hearing Jamie and Ed cheering in the background and banging their empty glasses repeatedly on the bar.

She enjoyed the feel of his arms about her. Breaking away reluctantly after kissing his cheek, she stayed with her arm linked loosely through his as they stood side by side and watched the band play their second set.

CHAPTER 38

"WE'VE SEEN SUCH a transformation in Peter since he's known you; just to be all together again and for it not to be Christmas is unheard of for a start."

"Daphne; you, William and Peter have made a big difference to my life. I thought I'd be spending the winter sitting alone in this cottage, but in such a short space of time we seem to have all become firm friends." Lyn smiled as she handed the older woman a jug of hot gravy to take into the dining room.

"I wouldn't be surprised if Peter pops the question one of these days. He's that smitten with you." Daphne took the jug and chuckled.

"I was married for thirty five years. I enjoy Peter's company, but really have no inclinations towards ever getting married again. One man was enough for me." She ensured that she had stated her case firmly enough for Daphne to grasp the message.

"Well, I for one hope you change your mind." Daphne turned towards the dining room.

Lyn rolled her eyes heavenwards, mouthed an expletive at Daphne's retreating back, and wondered why a woman could not just be friends with a man without somebody asking when they were going to be wed. She decided to have a quiet word with Peter later on about it before he went home, so that he could nip any more rumours in the bud before they got out of hand.

"Thank you for the superb meal, my dear. The lamb was cooked to perfection."

She smiled as Peter unfolded his jacket in what she supposed was the same way he had put on a coat since time immemorial. Giving the whole garment a shake, he carefully put in his left arm before following through with his right, and then smoothed it down at the front with the palms of both hands before doing up the buttons.

"Peter, I think I ought to mention something that Daphne said to me tonight."

"Mention away Lyn; I'm listening." He took his car keys from his pocket and then gave her his full attention.

"Er.........not to put too fine a point on it; she's started to go on about how I've made you very happy and that you'll be 'popping the question' soon."

"Oh dear."

"That's what I thought. I've already explained to you that I cannot have an intimate relationship with a man, and that I'm just looking for friendship."

"Of course. Me too. I'm as impotent as a roomful of eunuchs. My incompetent urologist has seen to that."

She tried hard to stifle a giggle, but failed.

"Sorry to laugh, but would you be able to let Daphne

and William know that we're just friends? It'll be kind of embarrassing to have to go through the same rigmarole every time I meet up with her."

"I'll try, but that's the trouble with Daphne; she gets a bee in her bonnet and she won't let it rest."

"Do your very best." She smiled and walked towards him. "Can a friend have a hug though?"

"I was hoping you'd say that." He opened his arms and she put her head on his shoulder. His jacket smelt of a rather pleasant aftershave.

"Dear Lyn; if we were only thirty years' younger. To twist Mr Binyon's words: 'Age has wearied them and the years condemned'. He sighed and kissed the top of her head.

"Speak for yourself; I'm only just starting out! Just because one part of us fails to work, it doesn't mean we've got to be written off like an old car!" She giggled again but kept her head on his shoulder.

"The piston's gone, and I may be only firing on three cylinders now, but I'm good for a few more years yet, my dear."

"Same here. We've got many more years of friendship ahead of us"

She broke away smiling.

"But without all those tedious animalistic tendencies; all that unseemly grunting and thrusting, it's so undignified."

She was still smiling as she closed the door behind him.

CHAPTER 39

"JAMIE, IF YOU and Sara start over on that wall; I'll do this one, and Peter, perhaps you can start in the kitchen?"

"Aye aye, Cap'n." Peter saluted as he picked up a paintbrush.

With the end of the cold weather in sight, Lyn's spirits had lifted with the arrival of Spring. She hummed as she opened one of the tins of magnolia paint that had been sitting unused in her hallway for months. The café would be open for business within a few weeks, and her days would soon be full again. She felt her energy levels rising with the knowledge that she would be her own boss, running her own business, and it felt good knowing she would be self-employed and productive at an age when some people were beginning to think about retiring. She had already made the first of many visits to the wholesalers to introduce herself, and had re-read Maureen's email several times advising her on the amount of goods she would need to order.

"How about the ceiling? Shouldn't we be doing that first?" Jamie, practical as ever, looked upwards.

"You're probably right. I've got some white emulsion here." She handed over a tin. "There's a ladder out the back, but we'll have to move the tables and chairs somewhere else though."

"Let's move them outside for now. It won't take long."

"I'll give them a wipe down while Jamie's doing the ceiling." Sara wedged open the door to the café and peered outside. "The weather's holding; they won't get wet."

"Thanks so much for your help all of you. The café's going to look great when we've finished. I've got someone from the carpet shop coming to lay some new lino tomorrow to finish it off."

"Just as long as I get a free cup of tea on opening day." Jamie stirred the contents of a tin of emulsion with a large screwdriver. "When is the big day by the way?"

"Easter Saturday. I can't wait!" Lyn sighed with anticipation.

"We'll be there, don't worry."

"And me!" Peter's voice came from the direction of the kitchen.

"I can help you out for a few weeks in the kitchen while I'm in-between jobs if you like." Sara looked at her questioningly.

"Great; thanks again everybody; I don't know what I would have done without you all." She smiled, "Come on Sara, let's get these tables and chairs outside."

Paint-spattered, with every joint aching, but also feeling extremely happy, Lyn looked forward to a long soak in the bath as she turned the Jag into the lane leading up to the cottage. Looking around her there were already signs that some of the other properties in the road were occupied, and she was comforted to know that at last there were some other people nearby. She thought back to how dark her days had been only a year previously, and she could hardly believe how much progress she had made in such a short time.

She sang along loudly to the radio until the sight of a white van parked in her driveway with oh-so- familiar lettering on the side caused her to pull the handbrake on suddenly and stop behind it in mid-song. With her happiness rapidly dissipating, she turned off the engine, got out of the car and walked up to the van. As she looked in the side window she was dismayed to see the sight of her ex-husband fast asleep in the driver's seat, mouth open and emitting snores loud enough to wake the dead. She felt irritated at his presence and yanked open the van door with more force than was necessary.

"Neil! What the hell are you doing here?" She poked a finger in the top of his arm, causing him to wake with a jolt.

"W-what's going on?" He yawned and rubbed his eyes. "Ah; you're here at last. I've been sitting in this bloody van for hours." He got out of the van stiffly and stretched.

"What do you want?"

"I've been driving all day and waiting around for you. I'm hungry, thirsty, and desperate for a piss."

"Oh God; I suppose you want to come in then. I hope you're not staying long; I want to get in the bath."

"Have a bath then and I'll cook us something to eat." He made his way to the front door. "What have you been doing? You're covered in paint."

"None of your business. There's a restaurant a few miles down the road if you want dinner. Other than that you can wait until I've had a bath and then I'm making myself a sandwich if you want one."

She turned the key in the lock, sighing with annoyance as Neil pushed past her and ran upstairs to the bathroom.

"A sandwich will be fine! I just need to have a piss first though before you get in the bath."

She slammed the front door, her joyful mood shattered with his arrival. Instead of her plan of soaking in an ocean of scented bubbles she knew it would now have to be a quick in-and-out shower, as she would not be able to relax until he had gone.

The television was blaring out when she came back downstairs wearing a clean sweatshirt and jeans, and rubbing her hair dry with a towel. To her added annoyance she felt the start of another hot flush creeping its usual path upwards from the centre of her chest.

"Didn't we ever get the Sky sports package?" She thought his voice sounded almost petulant.

"I stopped it; I can't stand looking at football. Why would I want to pay for something I don't use?" She saw with fresh irritation how he had made himself at home; stretching out on the settee as he had done in the old days. "Can you please turn the TV off; I can't hear myself think."

"Sorry; shall I make the sarnies? Your face is as red as a cherry." He stood up, pressing a button on the remote.

"I'll make the sandwiches. I've got cheese or ham until I go shopping tomorrow."

"Either. I'm not fussed. I'll make a cup of tea then to go with it."

She followed him out into the kitchen, boiling over with anger inside at the unwelcome intrusion.

"Neil; what are you doing here?" She opened the fridge and took out some ham.

"Oh, well, that's an easy one to answer; I've realised what a prat I've been. The past year has been a terrible mistake. I want to start afresh now and put it all behind us."

She wondered if she had heard him right. Lyn slammed the fridge door, and then closed her eyes and took in a deep breath, counting to ten before exhaling.

"How dare you waltz in here like nothing has ever happened! You turn my world upside down, and then just expect me to take you back and play cosy couples again? You must be out of your tiny mind!" She slammed the packet of ham down on the kitchen table and ripped open the loaf's cellophane packaging.

"Look; I'm trying to apologise here. I'm not with Janice anymore; she's gone back to her ex. Turns out the baby's his anyway; she'd been seeing him again on the side." He tried unsuccessfully to disguise the bitterness in his voice.

"So she's dumped you and I'm supposed to be eternally grateful and welcome you back with open arms then?" She felt strangely satisfied he now had an inkling of just what she had gone through. "Neil; I've made a life for myself here. It hasn't been easy but I've done it, and that life doesn't include you. I've got my own business now, and I've met a lovely man. It's over; you can't just drop me and expect to pick up where you left off. Life's not like that." She felt calmer having spoken her mind, and exhaled shakily as she spread margarine onto slices of brown bread.

"You've found somebody else?" He stared at her incredulously." You told me you can't have sex!"

"Nothing has changed. I still can't, but thank goodness I've found a kind person who doesn't care whether or not I can still perform the sex act. He likes me for myself. I'm treated like a lady, and when he's around I know I'm not just a vagina that's only been put upon the earth for the convenience of a man."

"Wow; he's either lying or he's gay then."

"He's neither; he's one in a million and I like him more and more every day." She enjoyed the look of undisguised jealousy and disappointment on his face.

"Well; I'm obviously in the way here. I'll have something to eat if you don't mind, and then I'll be off."

"Help yourself; there's some fruit cake afterwards if you want. I just needed to tell you how things are now. I know we were together for a long time, but the new normal is that I am post-menopausal, have no inclination for sex, and probably never will have the urge again. It happens to quite a lot of women my age. However; I'm dealing with it. I'm starting a new business on Easter Saturday; I'm taking over the café down on the Esplanade, and am reasonably happy now. If you came back the situation would be to your disadvantage, as you would have no sex life. I assume that's not what you want, so sooner or later you would stray again, and we would be back to square one. I can't set myself up for more hurt and misery; I've cut my losses and I'm surprised to say that despite everything I'm enjoying myself at last. There's life in the old girl yet, and sex isn't everything." She took a mouthful of sandwich, and smiled to herself as she imagined biting a large chunk out of his penis instead. "Anyway; you've never even once mentioned the most important word that a girl is looking for."

"What's that?" He stopped eating and looked at her with interest.

"Love."

CHAPTER 40

HER HEART WAS beating faster than usual as she turned around the 'closed' sign on the café door. *Had she ordered enough food from the wholesalers? Was there enough float in the till?* She pulled up the blinds and smiled, as the sound of clapping and cheering emanated from the direction of the kitchen.

"Woo hoo! She's done it! Well done Lyn!"

She turned on her heel and curtseyed, as Sara came out to the counter.

"We probably won't have a single customer all day."

"Of course we will! Jamie's coming in anyway, when he's finished the run to Exeter. And Peter's coming in for lunch, don't forget."

"That's two then. The beach is empty; no-one's about." She opened the door and looked up and down the Esplanade.

"Give it time; it's only ten o'clock in the morning."

"Make yourself a cup of tea whenever you want, Sara."

"Okay."

The delivery of a huge bouquet of flowers half an hour later took her by surprise as she finished serving her first customer. Opening the attached card she read the words that stopped her in her tracks momentarily.

Darling Lyn,

Please accept these roses with my good wishes for the successful start of your new career. I checked around, and as this was the only beach café opening at Easter I decided it must be your one (hope I was right?).

I've been thinking a lot about what you said when we last met. I've treated you terribly, and you have my admiration for starting from scratch and making a go of things. Amongst all the bad feeling and shit that's gone on I realise that I love you so much and I've never stopped loving you; you've been my rock for as long as I can remember. I can say from the heart that I've never been as miserable as I am now; to lose you and to know it's my own fault you've gone tears me up inside.

I never felt for Janice what I feel for you; I suppose you can say it was a mid-life crisis or something like that. She was 20 years' younger than me, and

I couldn't talk to her about films I've seen or music I love. Remember we were almost word perfect when watching 'Butch Cassidy and the Sundance Kid'? We loved that film, but Janice had never heard of it. She called me an old fart because I didn't know who Justin Timberlake was. Who the hell is he?

I've been such a stupid bastard; I've lost my house and I've lost my wife, who I now realise is the most important thing to me in the whole world. We had such good times, remember?

I'm renting a place in Truro now, not too far from you. I wanted to get away and make a whole new start. I have my health and my van, and I can find work anywhere. I'm beginning over again and am taking each day as it comes.

Good luck, love Neil. xxx'

The thought of him living only a half hour drive away was enough to send her good mood spiralling into a tailspin. She put the card in her pocket and took the bouquet out to the kitchen.

"Wow! What lovely roses! Who sent them?" Sara looked up from mashing some boiled eggs.

"My ex; Neil. Seems as though he's now living only about 20 miles away." She placed the flowers on the draining board still in their wrapping, and walked back towards the door.

"Ooh; watch out then. He might be keen to get back together. I'll find a vase and put them on the front windowsill for you."

"No way am I going to let him ruin my life again. He'll find somebody else before long anyway, and he'll realise I'm not what he's looking for."

As she went back out into the café, the door opened to reveal a familiar, smiling figure.

"Peter! Glad to see you. Whatever you're eating here is free today!" She kissed him on both cheeks.

"That's no way to make a profit, my dear." He returned the kiss, hitched up his trousers at the knees, and sat down at an empty table.

"You're an exception. What'll it be?" She moved out of the way as Sara came through carrying a vase.

"Just a toasted teacake and a pot of tea please." His eyes followed Sara. "What beautiful flowers! Where did you get them?"

"Neil sent them. I think he's feeling sorry for himself."

"So he should; so he should. Does this mean I am *persona non grata* then?" He stared at the roses with an unfathomable expression on his face.

"Peter, don't be silly. Neil is nothing to me now. I'll get you your teacake." She continued to talk to Peter while managing the small lunchtime flurry with ease, but by the time she greeted Jamie around three o'clock the café was empty.

"I'll have whatever's going off first. I'm starving!" Jamie took off his jacket and plonked himself down in a chair. "What, no customers?"

"We had a little flurry at lunchtime and Peter's been in, but then he had a rehearsal at the church for his Easter concert tomorrow."

"How's Sara doing; okay?"

"She's a little star. I hope she decides to stay actually"

"She's thinking about it. She likes the hours. She can never get up in the mornings, and not many jobs start at ten o'clock. We're saving up for a bigger house, and she's wondering about weekend work as well."

"I was going to advertise for somebody for the weekends, but of course Sara can come in if she likes."

"I'll tell her tonight and then she can make her mind up. What's going off?"

"Nothing yet fortunately. Sara's made a rather delicious quiche if you want some of that?"

"Real men don't eat quiche do they?"

"I won't say anything." She smiled and ruffled the top of his head.

She was pleased with the £62.47 profit from her first day's trading. After depositing the takings in the wall safe in her office, she locked the café; glancing once more as she did so at Neil's roses sitting in their plastic vase on the windowsill. She sighed. *She knew she could not be so churlish as to not thank him.* On returning home she switched on the computer, still remembering his email address:

'Dear Neil,

Thanks very much for the roses. My first day's trading has gone well; I've made over £62. Best wishes from Lyn.'

She did not want to say too much and encourage a response. Her conscience was clear, and she decided the short message would more than suffice. She sent the email and switched off the computer.

CHAPTER 41

EASTER SUNDAY DAWNED bright but chilly. She looked forward to meeting up with Peter for dinner later that evening at Daphne and William's after closing the café for the day. Sara was eager for the money and had volunteered her services over the bank holiday weekend, but Lyn still felt guilty at taking her away from Jamie. She logged into the computer early in the morning as she ate a bowl of cereal, finding with some surprise another email from Neil.

'My Darling Lyn,

So pleased you had a good first day at the café. I'm getting a few jobs in and around Truro now. I'm trying to pick myself up, but every night there's an empty spot on the right side of my chest where your head used to be. I wouldn't even mind if you tweaked my nipples again now (remember how I hated it when you used to do that?). I find that I have no interest in joining a dating agency or finding anybody else. I don't care about the sex anymore, it's the rapport we had and the common interests that I miss. What happened to us? All my love, Neil xxxxx'

She sighed and logged off. She had no interest in continuing the conversation.

By the time she had showered and dressed it was nine o'clock. As she put on her jacket prior to leaving the cottage, she thought she could hear footsteps on the driveway. Taking a glimpse through the spy-hole, to her horror she saw the same delivery man approaching carrying another large bouquet of flowers. The doorbell rang, and she opened it reluctantly.

"Delivery for Ms Fuller. Can you sign here please?" He gave her a leery look as he pushed a piece of paper and a pen into her hand. "He's keen; whoever he is."

"Thanks." She kept her face expressionless as she took the flowers, and was in two minds whether or not to throw the card in the bin unread. However, curiosity overcame her:

'My darling Lyn,

I just couldn't resist sending you another bouquet. I'm going to make it up to you for what I did. All the lies and the womanizing have stopped, and I'm living the life of a monk here; I'm even thinking of having one of those funny haircuts. I feel good; the sex was like an addiction, but I find I'm not interested now. Please come back to me and give it another try? We go back nearly 40 years; you knew me before I was even shaving properly. I don't know what to do without you. Love Neil.xxxx'

There was no time to respond to the message; she needed to go to work. Lyn left the bouquet untouched in the kitchen sink and walked briskly along the Esplanade, waving as she saw Sara in the distance sitting on the sea wall outside the café.

"Sorry I'm a bit late; he sent another bunch of flowers. I am at a loss to know what to do about it all." She sighed as she unlocked the door.

"Tell him to piss off; that usually works." Sara laughed as she jumped down from the wall.

"I don't think it will this time."

"Shall I send Jamie and Ed round?"

"I don't even know where he lives; just somewhere in Truro." She pulled up the blinds and turned around the 'closed' sign on the door.

"Tell him you're marrying Peter, or get a restraining order out on him."

"I don't want to marry Peter, and Neil's not come anywhere near me recently. He's playing a different game; it's like he's wooing me from afar."

"I would have liked to be wooed. You know what Jamie's like; all wham, bam and not even a thank you Ma'am."

"He loves you though. Anyone can see that. My husband loved me so much he went off with another woman." Lyn gave a hollow laugh as she made her way to the office.

"Shall I start by putting a batch of scones in the oven? We can do some cream teas today." Sara deftly changed the subject, switched on the light in the kitchen, and flicked the oven on to warm up.

"Sure. And perhaps take another chocolate gateaux out of the freezer. It seemed quite popular yesterday."

Word had obviously got about that the café was open, and business was brisker than the day before. She had no time to ponder on her ex-husband's strange behaviour until she returned home, pleasantly fatigued on earning more than double the first day's takings. The bouquet of flowers still lay in the sink where she had left it that morning, and with a sigh she set about arranging them in a vase. Before showering and dressing for her evening out she reluctantly logged into Outlook and checked her emails. *Nothing.*

What was he playing at? She found their last conversation and hit the 'reply' button:

'Neil, please stop sending the flowers. If I remember rightly we had a phone conversation about this time last year. You told me you didn't love me anymore. This all makes no sense. Lyn.'

"Is he becoming a nuisance, my dear?"

Lyn took the pot of vegetables from Peter, helped herself to broccoli and carrots, and then passed it on to Daphne.

"It's like he wants to carry on as if nothing's happened. He's full of remorse, and blames it all on a mid-life crisis. He's living in Truro now, but sooner or later I know he'll be turning up on my doorstep again."

"I'd have nothing more to do with him. You're just stirring up trouble for yourself all over again." Daphne took some carrots and handed over the pot to William.

"Yes; I know you're right Daphne. I've told him to stop sending flowers. We'll see if the message sinks in. If not, I'll just have to get a bit firmer with him."

"Call the police if he's harassing you." William poured gravy onto his Yorkshire pudding.

"And tell them my ex-husband keeps sending me bunches of flowers? Hmm; I can just see their faces when I relate that little gem." Lyn sighed. "This roast chicken is delicious, Daphne. You must give me the recipe for the stuffing."

She found a letter with a Truro postmark lying on her doormat when she returned home from work the very next day. She rolled her eyes to the heavens as she recognised the handwriting.

'Silver Birches

Lane End

Truro

'My darling Lyn,

You can delete emails without reading them, but I hope you'll open this letter. I received your email asking me to stop sending you flowers. I apologise if I've offended you, but I just wanted to do something nice for you instead of lying, cheating, and generally being the awful pain in the arse that I was a year ago. I've had plenty of time to think about the hurt and sorrow I've caused you, and if I could turn back the clock a few years I would do so. However, I can't do that and have to live with what I've done.

I love you with all my heart, and so desperately want to get back what we once had. I swear I've changed for the better. I've done doing the middle-aged fling thing, and believe me it can't compete with the stability of 35 years of marriage to (I realise now it's too late) the kindest and most wonderful wife that a man could have ever had.

You're in my thoughts night and day. I will love you forever.   Neil. xxx'

She wiped away a stray tear and put the letter in the top drawer of her desk for safekeeping. She tried unsuccessfully to think of any occasion during their marriage when she had received such lovely words from him.

CHAPTER 42

"REGGIE'S LOOKING FOR work, Lyn. Do you need her at all?"

Lyn wondered whether to take Reggie up on her offer. She glanced at Sara as she unlocked the door to the café.

"I could do with the help now the season's getting underway and we're a bit busier, but isn't her appearance a little..........er..........bohemian?" She brought to mind the two-foot long dreadlocks, the Doc Marten boots, the nose ring, and the 'ethnic' cheesecloth clothing.

"It can be. Tell you what; I'll have a word with her and tell her to smarten up her act if she doesn't want to frighten the customers away."

"Failing that she can work in the kitchen and you can help me serve." She pulled up the blinds and turned the 'closed' sign around.

"That might be better. She can be a little fiery, but she's got a heart of gold really. By the way, any more bouquets of flowers recently from you-know-who?"

"No, funnily enough everything's stopped; no emails, no flowers, and no letters. In fact nothing for a week."

"That's what you want though isn't it?" Sara walked between the tables and chairs on her way to the kitchen.

"Of course. Perhaps he's given up at last." Lyn hung up her jacket in the office and tried hard to keep the disappointment out of her voice. *Let him play his little games; she was having nothing to do with it.*

"Shall I tell Reggie she can start then?" Sara called from the kitchen.

"Okay. I'll give her a month's trial. Tell her to start on Monday at ten. Is she still with Joanie?"

"Oh yes; those two seem quite settled now." "Good."

She looked downwards to the doormat on arriving home that evening, but there was still no mail stamped with a Truro postmark. She took off her shoes, made herself a cup of tea, and tried to figure out what her ex-husband was up to. *Had he found another poor cow to bedazzle with his charm?* She shrugged her shoulders and took her cup out onto the patio. Sinking gratefully into a comfortable deckchair, she raised her face to the sun and closed her eyes.

The doorbell rang.

Sighing with irritation, she heaved herself out of the chair and padded barefoot to the front door. On opening the door wide, her mouth formed a little 'o' of surprise.

"Neil! What on earth are you doing here?" She looked him up and down, and thought he had definitely lost weight since she had last seen him.

"Can I come in?"

He was unsmiling. She noticed his pale complexion, and the unusual way that he was dressed from head to toe in black.

"I suppose so. Come in then." She closed the door behind him. "I was just sitting out on the patio. Do you want a cup of tea?"

"That'll be great, thanks." He walked through to the garden, and when she brought his tea she found to her annoyance he had sat himself back in her favourite deckchair that she had just vacated.

"To what do I owe the pleasure today?" She tried to keep the sarcasm out of her voice as she dragged another chair out from inside the shed.

"Dad's gone, doll. He died a couple of days' ago. I've been with Mum this week, sorting out the funeral arrangements." He looked down into his cup.

"Oh; I'm so sorry to hear that. I always liked the old boy." She spoke truthfully, hoping he would remember the genuine affection she had always felt for her ex father-in-law.

"My whole life has gone tits up." He sighed, closed his eyes and leaned forwards, putting his right elbow on his knee and leaning his forehead against his right hand.

"Was he ill? He'd always seemed so fit to me." She was slightly disconcerted by his unhappiness, and suddenly felt guilty for possibly having caused him more distress on top of having to cope with his father's demise.

"Throat cancer. He'd always liked a drink as you know; the doc reckoned that probably did it. He was gone a few months after being diagnosed. I came to ask if you wanted to go to the funeral next week. "

As she looked at him she saw a sea of unshed tears, and was loathe to add any more grief on top of the load he was already carrying.

"Of course I'll go. Give me the details and I'll be there."

"Can I drive you? It'll be at Eltham crematorium next Thursday afternoon. They're still in the same house in Bexley, so it'll be a long drive."

"Okay. I've got some help in the café now."

"Thanks, doll. Thanks a lot." He leaned back again in the chair, closed his eyes, and was fast asleep in seconds.

She took the empty cup from his hand and felt like crying herself; she had never seen him looking so utterly spent and miserable.

CHAPTER 43

"DON'T WORRY; REGGIE and I will be fine. I'll lock the takings in the safe at the end of the day tomorrow; you just do what you have to do." Sara gave a tablecloth one last wipe, as Lyn pulled the blinds down and locked the door.

"I've got to head into town now and find something black to wear."

"Do you think he's doing all this to win your sympathy and get you to go back to him?"

Lyn remembered how close Neil had been to his father, and shook her head.

"No; he's genuinely upset I can tell, as well as being full of remorse and guilt about going off with somebody else. By the way, Peter phoned last night and asked me the same question." She gave a little chuckle. "I told him not to fret, and that he couldn't get rid of me that easily."

"He's such a nice man; if only he was thirty years' younger!" Sara laughed. "I'll go and help Reggie finish up in the kitchen."

"She's doing okay. She's even tied her dreadlocks up so they don't fall in the food!" Lyn smiled, glanced through the serving hatch, and watched Reggie as she unloaded the dishwasher.

"Her feet must get hot in those diver's boots though." "Each to his own."

"New car? It's very comfortable." She liked the cosy feel of the BMW's leather seat. As she sat next to him and listened to his voice it seemed like old times; she could close her eyes and it was as if the past year had never happened. As though for a reality check she just had to look down at the bare ring finger of her left hand, to the white mark her wedding band had made that was now almost eradicated.

"You can adjust it so it fits your back perfectly. It's great isn't it?" He turned onto the A30 and picked up speed. "Thanks so much for coming today. It'll mean a lot to Mum, and it means a lot to me."

"As I said before, I always liked Stan." She looked at his hands on the steering wheel; hands so familiar to her that she still recognised every mole and freckle. He was quite naturally not wearing his wedding ring, and she briefly wondered what he had done with it.

"Do you remember at our wedding he got absolutely shit-faced?"

"Oh yes. He was laying in the doorway as I recall, and everybody had to step over him to go to the loo." She smiled at the long-ago memory.

"Mum was so embarrassed. I don't think she spoke to him for a fortnight."

"Before he passed out he told me that his son had married a good'un." She said it almost without thinking, and immediately could have kicked herself. She felt her heart pick up speed, and then the start of a hot flush.

"I certainly did. It's just that it took me thirty five years to realise it."

She was aware he had turned to look at her, but she kept her eyes firmly on the road ahead and tried to think of something to change the subject.

"Can we turn up the air-con please? I've got a sweat on." She puffed and panted as she tried to struggle out of her jacket without taking off the seat belt.

"Sure. You're still getting the flushes then?" He took one hand off the steering wheel to adjust the temperature control.

"They could go on for another twenty years I've been told. Can we stop for a wee and a coffee at Exeter before we get on the M5?"

"Okay. The funeral's not until four o'clock, so we've got plenty of time. I'm sorry I wasn't very sympathetic." He overtook a slow-moving caravan with ease. "Bloody caravans; I hate them."

"Sympathetic about what?" She turned towards him with interest.

"Your hot flushes and the whole menopause thing. I looked it up on Google. I didn't realise what you were going through. I suppose I tried to laugh it off as though it wasn't happening."

"Oh, it's happening alright. Some mornings it takes at least an hour and a hot shower before my joints stop aching. It sucks." She sighed and wiped the sweat away from the side of her nose.

"I didn't want to know. I just wanted us to stay the same as we always were."

"Nothing stays the same, Neil. Sometimes things change for the better, and sometimes for the worse."

"I've worked that one out. It's taken the worst year of my life to realise I've changed for the better."

"Glad to hear it."

"We're coming up to the Services. Do you still want to stop?"

His voice woke her abruptly from a doze. She remembered how annoyed he always used to be if she needed to stop on long car journeys. Knowing he always liked to drive straight on without stopping, she yawned and stretched while waiting for the inevitable moaning and groaning to commence.

"Yes please, if you don't mind."

"Sure. I don't mind at all."

He was calm and collected. When the BMW slid into a parking space she was most surprised when he jumped out and ran round to open the passenger door for her.

"Neil, you don't have to do that. I'm not the Queen for God's sake."

"Shut up. I'm enjoying treating you like one." He smiled as he activated the central locking system.

"So who are you then…King Kong?"

"I'm an arsehole; King of the Arseholes in fact."

"What a bummer!" She laughed and walked by his side towards the café.

CHAPTER 44

"THANKS FOR THE coffee. I'm awake again now."

She sipped the hot latte and reflected on the many occasions she had sat with him in motorway service cafes just like they were doing today, but instead they would have been on their way either to or from Cambridge for IVF treatment. They would have sat at similar tables to the one they were presently occupying, not awkward in each other's company, but full of hope for the repeat procedure she was about to undergo. She remembered he would more often than not be silent; doing a grand job of somehow listening to her nervous chatter, but actually not really hearing anything she said at all. Much later when she eventually felt the menstrual cramps that signalled the start of another period, he would hold her tight until she was all cried out.

She looked up from the frothy bubbles to find him smiling.

"Penny for them."

"Oh; nothing really. I was thinking about Stan and the time he shinned up our drainpipe when we were out because your mum was desperate for the loo." She hoped the lie sounded convincing.

"The neighbours saw him climbing in the bathroom window and called the police. Happy times." Neil chuckled and stirred in another sugar cube to his cup of coffee. "When did it all start to go wrong, doll?" His voice suddenly sounded plaintive amidst the ordinary chatter of several families seated nearby, and as she drank her coffee she had to look away from his gaze.

"Who knows? Time changes us I guess. We're not the same people that we used to be way back when. You wanted what I couldn't give you." She kept her eyes fastened down on the table.

"Did you blame me for not being able to give you a child? Was that when the rot started to set in?"

She saw his hand tremble slightly as he lifted his cup; he seemed frailer and somehow vulnerable. Gone was the usual bravado and swagger, and she wondered if he was on the verge of tears.

"I wasn't thinking about babies, but now you've mentioned it, if anything I always blamed myself. I always had that ideal picture fixed in my head of a mother, father and two smiling children. I felt inadequate for years; somehow less of a woman because I couldn't give you that scenario. But hey, it's all water under the bridge now; we'd better think about getting back on the road again soon if we're to get to the funeral in time."

They swallowed the last of their coffee and walked back to the car in silence, each deep in their own thoughts. She heard him sigh as he steered the BMW down the slip road to the M5.

"How could I have been so stupid as to lose you? Dad was right; he told me last year I was an absolute prat." He sniffed and picked up speed to join the flow of traffic.

"You had a male menopause to coincide with mine. I think it's a very common occurrence from what I've read." Lyn gave a rueful smile. "I always thought it was something that happened to other people, but I was wrong." She exhaled and kept her gaze on the open road.

"You've got someone haven't you?" He glanced at her with interest.

"I still have my good friend, Peter. We're not lovers; we're more like companions, but I'm very fond of him."

There was no immediate reply, but she could feel his tension rising as the car sped effortlessly along the outside lane. Finally she heard him clear his throat and seemingly hold his breath:

"Would you ever consider coming back to me?"

She had known that sooner or later he would ask the question, but she had prepared herself.

"Neil; you're not only grieving for the loss of your father, you're also depressed about our divorce, the break-up of your relationship with Janice, and the shock about the baby. These are not things you can recover from quickly. When you're in a happier frame of mind I know you'll want a full intimate relationship with a woman again, which I can't give you, and so we would be back to square one. I'm so sorry but I can't set myself up to be let down again; once is enough." She stated the well-rehearsed answer firmly, and tried to blank out any emotion which might have caused her voice to tremble.

The road signs flashed past in the blink of an eye. She gave up waiting for him to speak, and it was not until London and the M4 were only ten miles away that he surprised her with his reply.

"I'm going to insist on a paternity test. If Janice doesn't agree then I'll go through the courts. I don't think her ex-husband is the father. I think I am."

"What?" She was not sure if she had heard him right.

"I think I'm the baby's father. I've thought long and hard about this, and I'm sure he came back on the scene after she was already pregnant."

"Well, you can't be absolutely sure of course." She remembered only too well how clever Neil had been in covering up his affair.

"I'm sure. I'm going to find out."

"Was it a boy or a girl?"

"I heard she had a boy. If he's my son I need to know." He lapsed into silence again to negotiate the heavy traffic on the M4, and she was glad that his attention had been diverted. By the time they had exited the M25 onto the A2 it was early afternoon and her stomach was growling with hunger.

"Mum will have prepared some lunch. We're nearly there now."

She saw the familiar signs to the Black Prince Interchange. The sight of the pub brought back so many poignant memories of their courting days that she had to close her eyes until they had turned off and passed it by.

"I wonder if that's still the same table outside the front there?" He quickly glanced at her and grinned.

"Probably not; it would have got woodworm by now." She sighed and fought back the urge to smile.

"Wow; look at all the flowers, doll."

As they approached the house she saw that the whole front garden was full of wreaths and bouquets of flowers. She noticed a few family members and friends standing around in the garden.

"There's Uncle Jeff; Christ, he's got old." Neil pulled up on the opposite side of the road, got out of the car and waved to an elderly man standing on the front porch.

"He'll probably say the same about us."

"I'm not ancient; speak for yourself."

Feeling awkward at meeting the family once again, Lyn hung back and kept quiet other than exchanging the usual pleasantries. However, she was unprepared for the warmth of her ex- mother-in-law's greeting.

"Lyn! I'm so glad to see you! Please help yourself to some lunch. It's all on the table in the kitchen."

"Hi Maggie; it's great to see you again, although the circumstances could have been better." She smiled and hugged the little woman, who seemed to have shrunk even more.

"Neil said he was going to ask you to come. I never thought you'd say yes though."

"You and Stan were always good to me. There was no way I'd miss it." She saw tears in the older woman's eyes.

"It was a blessed relief when he died; he was in so much pain. He'd lost so much weight I had to buy boys' pyjamas for him."

"Don't cry, Maggie. Remember how he used to be. Keep that memory in your heart."

She felt her eyes fill up. The gaping absence of her ex father-in-law, combined with the familiarity of the house and Neil's presence all sent signals to her brain that she should somehow still be married. Any more words were unnecessary, and she found herself floundering in a sea of nostalgia and regret. It suddenly seemed only natural to feel Neil's arm hugging her close at the same time as he reached around his mother's shoulders with the other.

CHAPTER 45

THEY STOOD SILENTLY under the archway as the undertakers opened up the back of the hearse. As the coffin was lifted out with Maggie's wreath of lilies on top, Lyn thought how small it seemed for once such an exuberant, larger-than-life man. She was aware that Neil had bowed his head, and she instinctively slipped her hand in his, feeling him giving her fingers a little squeeze of gratitude.

The chapel was full. She took her place on the first pew next to Neil and his mother, still holding his hand. There was nothing else to do but to look at the coffin as it sat on a catafalque in front of a pair of closed purple velvet curtains that reached from floor to ceiling. All around her people shifted uncomfortably in their seats, coughing and waiting for the service to begin, while Nat King Cole crooned 'Unforgettable' in the background. The minister appeared, coming to stand before them on a small plinth.

"For we brought nothing into this world, and it is certain we can carry nothing out; nor will we need worldly substance after death, any more than we did before we were born. The

Lord giveth, and the Lord taketh away. Blessed be the name of the Lord."

She was aware that Maggie had begun to cry. She let go of Neil's hand as he pulled his mother towards him.

"We are gathered here today to give thanks for the life of Stanley John Fuller. Many of you would have known him in his capacity as a tireless fundraiser for our local hospice. Some of you would have worked with him at the brewery, but to Maggie and Neil he was just a much loved husband and father. Stanley loved music, and we shall begin our service today by singing his favourite hymn 'I Vow to Thee, My Country'".

Gustav Holst's music filled the chapel, and caused a shiver to run down her spine. Lyn wanted Stan to jump out of his coffin, join in with the hymn he loved so much, and ask in his own inimitable way why everyone was pissing about. However, the lid of the coffin stayed firmly closed, and the mood remained sombre. Stan was gone; one of the few people in the world who had really loved her. Her eyes brimmed with unshed tears for her father-in-law, for her ruined marriage, and for Neil; hell-bent as he was on chasing the elusive prize of fatherhood.

"Maggie wishes me to recite 'A Song of Living' by Amelia Josephine Burr. It sums up Stan's love for life and for his God. The minister adjusted his spectacles and read from a handwritten sheet.

"Because I have loved life, I shall have no sorrow to die.

I have sent up my gladness on wings, to be lost in the blue of the sky.

I have run and leaped with the rain, I have taken the wind to my breast.

My cheek like a drowsy child to the face of the earth I have pressed.

Because I have loved life, I shall have no sorrow to die.

I have kissed young love on the lips, I have heard his song to the end.

I have struck my hand like a seal in the loyal hand of a friend.

I have known the peace of heaven, the comfort of work done well,

I have longed for death in the darkness and risen alive out of hell.

Because I have loved life, I shall have no sorrow to die.

I give a share of my soul to the world where my course is run.

I know that another shall finish the task I must leave undone.

I know that no flower, nor flint was in vain on the path I trod.

As one looks on a face through a window, through life I have looked on God.

Because I have loved life, I shall have no sorrow to die".

There did not appear to be a dry eye in the house. All around her Lyn could hear the sounds of weeping and sniffing into handkerchiefs. Neil, head bowed, wiped his eyes with the back of his sleeve, and sought the comfort of her hand with his own. She exhaled a shaky breath and watched as rays of sunlight broke through the stained glass window and shone down onto the sleek wood of the coffin.

"In the immortal lines of William Wordsworth, another of Stan's favourites:
Though nothing can bring back the hour
Of splendor in the grass, of glory in the flower;
We will grieve not, rather find
Strength in what remains behind."

The minister took off his spectacles and addressed the congregation:

"After our second hymn, 'Lead Us, Heavenly Father, Lead Us', we will then say The Lord's Prayer together."

The congregation could not be heard singing at all over the booming basso profundo of the minister's voice, and Lyn was aware that Neil had remained silent throughout the hymn. As she recited the comforting words of The Lord's Prayer she was glad she had made the journey to say goodbye to her father-in-law. It felt somehow right for her to be there, and although she was no longer a part of the family, after 35 years she knew there had definitely been a small place in his heart set aside for her.

"We now commit his body; earth to earth, ashes to ashes, and dust to dust, in sure and certain hope of the resurrection to eternal life."

The curtains opened, and the coffin moved silently on well-oiled wheels into infinity. Lyn felt her hand being gripped tighter and she heard a small sob emanating from her ex-husband's lips. She moved closer to him as he let go of her hand, putting one arm around her shoulders and the other around his mother. He sat between them and cried like a baby. Lyn put her head on his shoulder and as she wept it crossed her mind to wonder if the death of his father might not be the only thing that was upsetting him so much.

"Let's have a look over there. Someone said there's a nice pond and places to sit." Neil began to walk towards a sign that pointed to the Garden of Remembrance.

Leaving the other mourners commenting on the many wreathes, Lyn followed him down a concrete path that led to the garden. He found a seat in the sunshine next to a trickling fountain, flopped down and exhaled loudly while drying his eyes with a handkerchief and loosening his black tie.

"Thank Christ that's over." His voice sounded shaky with emotion.

"It couldn't have gone better. Maggie will be pleased." Lyn was aware he had put his arm around her again. "We can't stay here for long; the limousines will want to leave soon I expect."

"I just wanted to say thanks for your support today." He pulled her closer and kissed the top of her head. "I love you, Lyn. I'll always love you until I go through those bloody awful purple curtains myself."

She did not want to cause an argument and tell him not to kiss her while he was so emotionally upset. She sat peacefully with her head on his shoulder, ignoring another hot flush. It seemed quite like old times. She listened to the fountain playing its watery tune, and was quite disappointed when somebody sought them out and announced it was time to go.

She sat next to him in the hearse on the short journey back to Bexley, and found he had linked his fingers in hers.

As she felt the warmth of his hand, she thought that it seemed somehow right for them to be together on such an occasion.

212

CHAPTER 46

"PLEASE STAY TONIGHT. I've got the two spare rooms; one downstairs next to the shower room, and one upstairs next to mine in case you've forgotten. You're both welcome of course; you can't drive back all that way twice in one day." Maggie smiled at Lyn as she loaded the dishwasher after the last mourner had left.

"I had booked into a local bed and breakfast, but Neil will need to drive me there as I'm not insured to drive his car."

"Then you must stay, as Neil's had a few beers. What do you say Neil?"

"If it's okay with Lyn, then it's okay with me. She can have the downstairs room; it's bigger and it's got a double bed." He collected up the last of the plates from the dining room and brought them into the kitchen. "What do you want doing now, Mum?"

"Nothing really. I'm tired: I'm going to have a nice bath, go to bed, and have a clean around tomorrow."

"Okay, we'll have a sit in the garden and then we'll have a shower so as not to keep you awake."

"Night night, both. Thanks so much for coming, Lyn."

"I'm glad I did. See you in the morning Maggie." Lyn turned off the light in the kitchen and walked through to the garden.

"Poor old Mum; it's going to hit her hard in the next few months."

"She's a strong lady. She'll find a way of coping." She sat down on one of two wooden benches available, noticing how he came to sit close to her again.

"Fancy another cuddle? I sure as hell could do with one." He ripped off his black tie and threw it onto the grass.

"Neil; is this a good idea?" She assumed he would sit on the opposite bench.

"I think it's a very good idea. In fact, I'd go as far as saying it's the best idea I've had in a long while." He closed his eyes, leaned his head back, and put his arm around her. Lyn smelled beer and aftershave. His body felt comfortingly warm. She put an arm around his waist, rested her head on his shoulder, and listened to the dying birdsong.

"Come back to me, doll. We were good together." "Until you had your man-o-pause and went off with Pinky Pants."

"I've learned my lesson. I've already admitted I've been a prat."

"I don't want sex."

"I haven't asked you for any."

She pressed her face into his shirt front and giggled.

"I don't think it'll work."

"How do you know?"

"I just know. There's Peter now as well."

"What's he got to do with it? Tell him to sling his hook."

"He's my friend, Neil; a good friend."

"I hate the bastard."

"I'm going to have a wash." She stood up, irritated. "Can you get my stuff out of the car please?"

She felt better after her shower. While Neil was washing she sat in her nightdress on the edge of the bed and turned on her mobile phone, checking it for messages. There was only one:

'Hope the funeral went well. Looking forward to seeing you tomorrow. Peter x'

She sighed.

"Is that him sending you messages?"

She looked up from the phone to see her ex-husband standing in the doorway, naked from the waist up and wearing just his pyjama bottoms.

"Yes, if it's any business of yours."

"How will we ever get back together if he's always in the way?"

"Who said we're getting back together?"

"Well; there's a chance isn't there?" "I don't know."

"At least that's better than the 'no' I usually get." He came into the bedroom, closed the door, and stood in front of her, smiling.

"Neil......."

The sight of his flesh brought back a thousand pleasant memories. The temptation to sink her face into the comforting warm, hairy place she knew in the middle of his bare chest was overwhelming. Further down a telltale bulge beginning to grow beneath his pyjama bottoms proved to her that he possibly thinking along similar lines.

"Look what you're doing to me." His voice was thick with emotion.

"I can't have sex. You know that. Nothing works anymore." Her heart picked up speed, and a hot flush seeped across her face. She silently cursed her advanced age and her bodily infirmities.

"You said a long time ago that there were other ways. Perhaps now's the time to find out what they are."

She had a sudden urge to wipe out all traces of another woman, and claim her rightful place back in his heart. Gently lowering his pyjama trousers as he stood there, her hands reached around to his buttocks and her tongue traced a slippery line along the length of his penis:

"Oh God; you don't know how good that feels." His head tilted back and his eyes closed in rapturous ecstasy.

She was glad she had been curious enough to sit through many late night TV programmes on sex tips for the dissatisfied. She recalled all of the participants had been younger, and not one had suffered with her exact problem, but despite this she had carried on watching and learned how to give the best oral sex a man could ever want. She never thought she would ever be dredging up that particular store of knowledge again, but that night in her mother-in-law's house she called upon her menopausal memory to supply her with the information, and for once it did not let her down.

She awoke to the sound of cups rattling in their saucers. Neil lay on his side behind her; his arm was draped around her waist, and his leg felt heavy over her hip. Wriggling out from under his grasp, she turned to give her ex-husband a nudge.

"Your mother's in the kitchen making tea. Quick; put your trousers on and run upstairs, otherwise she'll see the bed hasn't been slept in. Mess it up a bit." She whispered frantically and prodded him in the chest.

"What? What's going on?" His arm came back around her waist and he lifted his leg over her body. She pushed it off with a sigh.

"Hurry up. She'll be knocking on the door in a minute to bring you a cup of tea."

"We've been married for thirty five years." He yawned and stretched. "She knows we sleep together."

"Not any more we don't. I don't want this going all round the family."

"If we don't sleep together any more, what am I doing in your bed then?" He gave her a grin and a leery look.

"Will you get a move on? I can hear her stirring hot water in the teapot."

"Oh, for fuck's sake!" He hopped out of bed and made for the door.

"Put your trousers on!" She hissed and stifled a giggle.

"Bollocks!" He ran back and picked up the pyjama bottoms, putting them on back to front in haste.

As he ran upstairs she leaned back against the pillow with the widest of grins upon her face.

There was no pressing need to make much conversation. Feeling comfortable with the silences, Lyn leaned back in her seat and enjoyed the effortless way in which the BMW ate up the miles back to the start of the M5.

"Will your mum cope okay on her own?" She felt guilty at leaving the elderly woman who had been so kind to her.

"She's got her brother and nephew and niece nearby with their families. I'll nip down and see her as often as I can. Oh, by the way, she'd already knocked on my bedroom door by the time I'd got up there this morning, because it was wide open."

"Oh shit; that'll get round now."

"So? Are you bothered?" He glanced quickly to his left, checking her expression.

"People will think what they want." She shrugged her shoulders and closed her eyes.

"I'd like to assume they'll think the same as me."

"What's that?" She knew the answer even before she asked the question.

"That we're getting back together."

"I don't know. As I said, there's no way I'll ever be able to have sex again; that's the problem." She opened her eyes and looked at him.

"So what were we doing last night? Peeling potatoes? I'm sure looking forward to having my spuds baked again if so…" He smiled as he overtook a lorry and settled back into the middle lane.

"I've made a different life for myself. I've got the café now."

"And *him*."

"We're good friends. He can't have sex either, and it suits me right down to the ground."

"So what do you do then? Talk about the weather?"

"Mind your own bizz." She touched her nose with the tip of her finger.

"It felt like old times with you in my arms. I haven't had a better night's sleep in ages."

"I should never have led you on. It was wrong of me." She sighed as she remembered the feel of his penis in her mouth.

"Lead me on any time you like. I wouldn't mind doing the same for you if you like." He chuckled and moved over to the left hand lane.

"Nothing works any more down below. You have to get that into your head."

"No harm in going through the motions though." He turned towards her and gave a wicked grin.

She worked hard on stifling a smile. *How did he always know how to make her laugh?*

When he dropped her off at the cottage she was in two minds whether to ask him in for a coffee, but at the last minute changed her mind in case he expected to receive a replay of the previous evening's spontaneous sex session. She had no idea what had come over her the day before, as she waved him off with a slight feeling of regret at being left alone again.

CHAPTER 47

"THANKS SO MUCH girls for holding the fort here for two days." Lyn unlocked the café door and looked about her appreciatively at the spotlessly clean floor and shining tables.

"No problem. Reggie has been an absolute star." Sara smiled at Reggie, who blushed.

"There'll be a little bonus in your pay packets this week."

"Thanks. It'll go towards some curtains for the new house. Jamie and I will be moving in as soon as the contracts are exchanged."

"Wow! Whereabouts are you moving to?" Lyn pulled up the blinds and turned around the 'closed' sign.

"We've got a semi about a mile from Jamie's old place. Mum and Dad helped us out with the deposit in the end. As soon as we move in we're having a housewarming party, and you'd better come."

"Of course! I look forward to seeing it." Lyn turned towards the office.

"How did the funeral go?" Reggie took off her hoodie, tied up her dreadlocks, and followed behind Lyn.

"As well as could be expected. He was a nice old boy, I was very fond of him." Lyn smiled as she opened up the safe and took out the float.

"Did you get on okay with your ex?" Sara stood in the office door with Reggie, both ready for a chat.

"Not too bad." She kept her face straight. "He wants us to get back together."

"No! He'll only do it again! You don't want to put yourself through that twice."

"I know; that's what I told him."

"Don't let him talk you round. You don't need him now."

"He seems so….what's the word….contrite? I've never seen anybody so sorry for what they've done."

"It's all an act. I had a bloke like that once. Within six months of me taking him back he was off dipping his wick again."

"Men. Useless bunch of pricks. Lyn, take my advice and find a woman; she'll never let you down." Reggie chuckled as she walked off towards the kitchen.

"I would if I could Reggie, but I'm afraid I'm not that way inclined!" Lyn shouted in the direction of Reggie's retreating back.

"Hello, my dear. One strong cup of tea please, if you don't mind"

Lyn kissed her friend on both cheeks.

"Peter! Lovely to see you! Have you been by the café while I was away?"

"No; I was waiting for you to return. You have been sorely missed."

"I needed to go and say goodbye to my ex father-in-law for my own piece of mind. He was a lovely man."

"Of course; of course. How did Neil treat you?"

"Very well. He wants us to get back together, but I was expecting that."

"What will you do?"

"Don't worry; it wouldn't be in my best interests to go back with him."

"I'm very glad to hear it. He sounds a downright scoundrel if you ask me." He sat down at an empty table, patted the empty chair next to him, and smiled up at her. "If you're not too busy, why not join me?"

"Okay, it's early yet. I'll grab a coffee."

"Don't worry Lyn, I'll bring it over with Peter's." Sara disappeared into the kitchen.

"Your rendezvous with the enemy, so to speak, has made me rethink a few things." Peter stirred his tea and replaced the spoon on the saucer.

"What things?" Lyn added a cube of sugar to her coffee.

"The fact is my dear, I don't want to lose you." "I'm not going anywhere."

"But there's a campaign going on by your ex-husband to win you back. I fear the battle will be lost without interventional strategies on my part."

"Eh?" She sipped her coffee, with one eye on a family who were reading the menu on a blackboard outside.

"I need to step up operations." He cleared his throat and looked over at her.

"Peter, will you just come out and say what it is you're trying to say?"

"My dear; I am not in the prime of life anymore, but I have come to the conclusion over the last two days that we would make good comrades in arms."

She looked at him uncomprehendingly.

"So it fills me with great nervousness and trepidation to ask such a question, but if you would give me the pleasure of becoming my wife, it would make me the happiest man alive." He took a small box from his pocket, and gave her a somewhat pleading look as he handed over the box and picked up his cup again to drink.

She stared at him open-mouthed in disbelief, then quickly opened the lid of the box to reveal a solitary diamond ring sparkling in white gold. When the café door opened to admit the first customers of the day, she gathered her senses, stood up quickly and gave him back the box together with a slightly over-zealous smile.

"Thank you so much for asking and for the ring, but I couldn't possibly answer you now. Give me a few days to think about it"

"As you wish, my dear. As you wish."

She walked home along the seafront, lost in thought. In the space of a couple of days the whole order of her life had been turned upside down again. Resigned to spending the rest of her days alone, she had clung to the lifeline of the café like a barnacle to a rock. The knowledge that two men were now locking horns over her was the most uplifting feeling in the world, and there was a spring in her step as she climbed down onto the beach and meandered along the shoreline.

But was Sara correct? Would Neil find somebody else eventually? Did she love Peter enough to marry him?

On reaching home she was surprised to find a bouquet of flowers propped up in a corner of the outer porch. She picked them up and sighed as she read the attached card.

'Thanks so much for being there for me. I will love you forever. Neil. xx'

Staring at the flowers on the kitchen table as she ate her evening meal, Lyn put forkfuls of food into her mouth automatically without really tasting anything. The choice she had to make was overwhelming and weighed heavily on her mind. *If she decided to remain single there was probably a lonely old age waiting for her just around the corner. On the other hand if she went back to Neil, the man she had loved since she was a teenager, there was the possibility he would stray again in the future if her technique in the bedroom was not good enough; therefore she would end up alone once more anyway. However, if she married Peter there would be no sexual demands, and the security of a comfortable old age with a companion she was fond of but did not love.*

She tossed and turned in bed, unable to sleep. Finally at 3am she made up her mind what she was going to do. She closed her eyes in relief at coming to a decision, and sank into a dreamless slumber until being woken up by the noise of the dustmen emptying the bins outside.

CHAPTER 48

"MY DEAR, I am the luckiest man in the world! We're going to have many happy years together."

She felt secure with Peter's arms around her, but knew she would probably wonder for the rest of her life whether or not she had made the right choice.

"I haven't told Neil yet, but he keeps asking if he can visit. I'll phone him, invite him round, and tell him then." She gazed at her new engagement ring glinting in the lamplight.

"Should I be there, do you think?"

"Probably not; he's a bit excitable. Perhaps go and see Daphne and William and let them know?"

"As soon as I tell her, Daphne will want to take over all the wedding arrangements."

"That's fine by me. I'm hopeless at all that sort of thing."

"May I kiss the bride? Of course it'll never go beyond kissing, but you already know that."

His kiss was passionless and as light as a butterfly's wings. Lyn felt strangely deflated while remembering Neil's tongue and his urgent kisses in her mother-in-law's spare room.

"Thanks for dinner tonight, Peter." She drew back from him and smiled.

"My cooking skills were never very formidable."

"Nonsense. The meal was fine." She picked up her bag. "I need to get home now though."

"Of course. Where shall we live when we're married?" He helped her on with her coat.

"I haven't thought that far ahead yet."

"Hey, doll! I've missed you so much!"

She felt herself encompassed in a familiar blanket of Neil. After gazing at him she thought he might have put on a few pounds. He also seemed much more contented.

"How's work?" She extricated herself from his clutches.

"Great. That's the beauty of my job; I can find work anywhere."

"Come in and I'll make you a cup of tea. I've got something to tell you."

"You and me both."

"Oh?" She moved down the hallway into the kitchen, hearing him following behind.

"You first." He pulled out a chair and sat down, putting a piece of paper from his pocket on the table in front of him.

"Peter's asked me to marry him, and I've said yes." She held her breath as she poured hot water from the kettle into the teapot.

The silence was almost tangible. She kept her gaze down on the two cups of tea as she brought them to the table. Finally she looked up as she heard him speak:

"You can't marry that prat!" He looked aghast and unbelieving, as he stared at her engagement ring.

"Why not? I can and I am. He's offering me security, loyalty, and companionship in my old age. I can do a lot worse."

"No you can't; you don't love him."

"What's love got to do with it? Even Tina Turner knows that." She smiled as she started to hum the chorus line.

"Everything. I love you and I know you love me. We've known each other since we were kids, for God's sake. Here; have a look at this." He shoved the piece of paper across the table.

"What is it?"

"It's the result of a DNA test. The baby's mine, doll. I'm a father!"

"What?" She wondered if she had heard him right as she scrutinised the words.

"Yeah, it's there in black and white! I've had to go through the courts to get that. Janice fought me all the way and now I've got to ask the judge to grant me access to my own child, but access I will get, you can depend on it." He had a triumphant expression on his face as he put the piece of paper back in his pocket. "Just imagine; we can be the family we always wanted to be, even if I do look like his grandfather and even if it's only every other weekend and two evenings a week!"

He was unstoppable and his enthusiasm was infectious.

"Come and sit on my lap, doll." He held out his right hand and picked up his cup of tea with the other.

"Neil; I'm marrying somebody else."

"No you're not. For Christ's sake come here." He pulled at her top and she fell into his lap.

"His name is Billy and he's three months' old. We can take him to the zoo on Sundays and queue up to see Father Christmas when he starts appearing in August. You can cuddle him when he falls over, teach him to read, and I can buy him a train set." He kissed her on the cheek and gave her a squeeze.

"His mother would be horrified if I did all that."

"She won't have a say in it; that's the best bit. It's all going through the courts, legal as anything."

"Oh, Neil. Why are you doing this to me? Why don't you just leave me alone?" She buried her head in his shoulder and sighed.

"Because I love you, and because this is the nearest we're ever going to get to being parents. You've waited a long time for this, doll. Don't turn it down; you'll never get another chance. It's all over with Janice, and there'll never be anybody else but you ever again. Come on, give me a 'yes'. You know you want to." He reached up and planted another kiss on her cheek.

"It's the sex issue, Neil. We'll be back to square one in a fortnight."

"What was wrong with that time at Mum's? If you don't want sex though you have my permission to cut it off with a rusty breadknife. Whatever you want; the ball's in your court. No, actually, my balls are in your court. Come on; give us a yes." He gave her one last squeeze for good measure.

"Okay; yes. Yes!" She laughed, wrapped her arms around his neck, and hugged him tight.

"Thank you so much, darling." He exhaled with relief. "One more thing; take that bloody ring off. I can feel it digging in my neck."

She took off the engagement ring and put it in her pocket, and all the while kissing him with a passion she never realised she still had.

CHAPTER 49

"YOU CAN'T DO that to the poor old boy!"

"Jamie; I can't help it. It's all working out with Neil now. We're going to give it one more try."

"Peter will be devastated. He loves you, I know."

Listening to Jamie's voice on the other end of the telephone, she was suddenly flooded with guilt and remorse.

"I was just using him as a security blanket, and that's not really fair on anyone. He needs to find somebody who loves him."

"I take it you haven't told him then?"

"No, not yet. I can't bring myself to do it."

"Do it soon, for both your sakes."

"I will. How's the move going?" "Contracts will be exchanged next Friday." "Give me a ring when I can come and visit." "Sure will. Bye for now." "Bye, Jamie."

As she hung up the receiver she sighed and dialed the number she knew off by heart.

"Hello Peter."

"Lyn! What a surprise! I was just thinking of you. Daphne wants to meet up to discuss wedding arrangements."

"Peter, can I pop over and see you tonight?"

"Of course! Shall I cook us something?"

"No, I'll eat before I get there. Shall we say seven o'clock?"

"Seven it is then. I'll look forward to it."

I won't.

Her heart was thudding away in her chest and the familiar hot flush crept over her face as she pulled up outside the detached house she had come to know so well in the last year. Before she was out of the car he was standing in the doorway, smiling and waving.

"It's so good to see you again, Lyn!" He gave her a gentle kiss as she walked up to him. "Come in, come in. I'm all yours for the evening. I'll put the kettle on."

She took off her jacket and put it down by the front door with her bag, wanting to make sure of its whereabouts for a quick getaway. While he was busy in the kitchen she paced impatiently up and down the front room, wanting to get the whole thing over with and be on her way.

"I remembered you don't have sugar." He came into the room and handed her a cup.

"Thanks, Peter. Look, I've come here tonight to tell you something."

"Then you must tell me, my dear. What is it? Do sit down. I'm all ears." He waved her towards a comfortable armchair.

"I hate to have to do this to you, but I can't marry you after all." Sitting down, she wanted to cry when she saw the hurt expression on his face. "I'm going to give it another try with Neil. I'll never know if he's changed unless I go back to him. We go back a long way; I love him. I'm so sorry." She held out the box to him containing the engagement ring.

"My dear, you are doing the wrong thing, but you must do what you must do. All I can say is that you will regret it. He will let you down again and again; that is one thing you can be sure of." He walked towards her, took the ring, and held it tight.

"Peter, one day you will find somebody who will want to wear that beautiful ring. I cannot marry you if I love somebody else. It's not fair to you. Again, I'm so sorry." She put her cup down and stood up.

"There is nobody else but you, my dear. The ring is for you in the future should you change your mind and wish to wear it. I shall wait for you to come back to me, as I know you will." He looked down at the box and sighed.

"I should go now."

"Of course."

Blinded by tears, she kissed him on the cheek and almost ran to the front door. She picked up her bag and jacket, feeling as though she wanted the ground to swallow her up whole.

"Goodbye, my dear." He stood erect and proud, but alone.

"Goodbye Peter."

CHAPTER 50

THE AUTUMN LEAVES swirled around outside Hayle's Registry office as Lyn, dressed in pale pink layered chiffon and holding onto her husband's arm, carefully negotiated the steps down to the garden area wearing her new pink four inch stilettos.

"Haven't we already got one of these?" Neil loosened his tie and held up a piece of paper in front of her.

"I cut it in half a long time ago, along with your leather trousers." She looked down at the pristine certificate of marriage in his hand.

"The waistband had shrunk anyway. I couldn't get the buggers on."

"Ah, so *that* was the reason!" She giggled and waited for their guests to assemble around them for the official photo.

"Give him a kiss, Lyn!" Jamie raised his camera.

"Hang on Jamie. Neil; quick: Do your tie up properly, it's photo-shoot time."

"Bloody hell, not another picture!" He grumbled as he secured the tie, and posed awkwardly.

"It's your wedding day. Smile and be jolly." Jamie waved his camera in the air.

"Up yours, Jamie."

She saw Cat and Caroline coming towards them. She thought Caroline, covered from head to toe in black silk, seemed rather oddly dressed for a wedding.

"Can I throw some confetti?" Caroline smoldered and drawled.

"Okay, but make sure Jamie's ready so that he can get a good photo."

"Who's that? One of the witches of Eastwick?" Neil shot Caroline a peculiar look.

"She's the drummer with an all-girl Led Zeppelin tribute band. Goes by the name of Joan Bonk'em." Lyn smiled and posed as Jamie snapped away.

"You don't say? That's my kind of lady!" Neil's eyes half closed against the shower of confetti.

"You're a married man again now. Anyway, she only likes the girls."

"She's giving me a funny look."

"I told you; she doesn't like men, and anyway she has her partner Reggie now."

"Reggie? I thought you just said she didn't like men?"

"She doesn't. Reggie's a girl." "Woop-de-do-dah."

"Great photo! Now, can you sit on his lap over there, Lyn?" Jamie pointed his finger towards a bench.

"Okay. Oh God; is that Peter sitting watching us? She turned to look at an all-too-familiar silver-haired figure sitting straight-backed on a seat in the far corner of the garden.

"He won't be stalking you for much longer once we move back down to Surrey." Neil stood and stared, stony faced with hands on hips, in the direction of the figure.

"Leave him alone. Come on; Jamie wants me to sit on your lap."

"Sounds like a good idea." He pulled her to him as he sat down. "Let's see what comes up."

"Doesn't it ever go down?" She wrapped one arm around his neck and smiled for the camera.

"No, never; it's a bloody nuisance."

"I'll hit it with something." She held up her marriage certificate and winked to the camera.

"Hit it with that big jar of your menopause cream in the bathroom. That'll do the trick." He laughed, squeezed her waist, and gave a little smile towards the camera.

"It's wild yam cream."

"Is it doing anything?"

"Not really."

"Where are you putting it?"

"None of your business."

"What a shame."

"I can't help it that nothing works. Get used to the new normal."

"I'm used to it already. I wouldn't want it any other way."

"Liar."

"Your hot flushes really turn me on. Who's that woman coming over?"

"That's Jamie's girlfriend Sara. She'll be running the café for me for the rest of the season, and then we'll see what happens next year."

"Hi Lyn! Lovely service! Can I take a picture of you to put on the café wall?" Sara stood in front of Jamie and grinned.

"One more photo and then we're done, I think. Neil's not going to pose for much longer; he's getting ready to blow a fuse."

"You can say that again." He whispered in her ear.

"Peter's over there, Lyn." Jamie turned and waved to the silent figure on the seat, who slightly raised his right hand in salutation. "I'll go and speak to him when you and Neil get in the car to go to the wedding breakfast."

"Okay, thanks. Tell him I'm sorry, but Neil wouldn't like it if I came over and spoke to him today."

"I'm sure he'll understand." Jamie put his camera back in its case and zipped it up. "Sara and I will jump on the bike and be with you as soon as we've spoken to Peter."

She watched her husband as he looked around the venue.

"Didn't you want something fancier for your wedding day? I mean; it's a bloody fish and chip shop! Look at Mum's and Uncle Jeff's faces; they can't believe it."

"Jamie's brother owns it. He's decorated it all nice for us. Show him a bit of appreciation." Lyn grinned and waved at the man pouring a container of raw chipped potatoes into the deep fat fryer. "You've done a grand job, Ed!"

"Cheers. Private party this afternoon! Frying plaice, cod or haddock, your choice!"

The hiss and sizzle of the chips made her feel hungry. As the few guests took their seats, Jamie and Sara pulled up outside on the bike, took off their crash helmets and came into the shop.

"Cod and chips twice please brother, and don't spare the vinegar!"

"Coming up!" Ed adjusted his apron and started to dip raw pieces of fish into a vat of batter.

"I'm so glad to have you back in the family again, Lyn." Maggie Fuller poured some salt on her chips and speared a few with her fork.

"It's like I've never left and this past year and a half has all been a dream." Lyn washed down her meal with a strong mug of tea and sat back in her chair. "I hope you weren't too shocked at the wedding. We did the meringue dress and a hundred and fifty guests the first time round as you remember. We wanted today to be simple and without fuss; so Neil left it to me, and this is my choice." She waved an arm around the shop. "These are all my friends. They have been good to me, and I wanted to give them all a day they'd enjoy. They wouldn't feel at home in a fancy restaurant, and come to think of it, neither would I now." She smiled at her mother-in-law.

"If only Stan could have seen you two together again." Maggie's eyes misted over at the thought.

"I'm sure he's looking down at us and eating a plate of chips in celebration." Lyn raised her mug and looked up towards the ceiling. "Here's to you, Stan!"

"I want to thank everybody for their cards and presents, and for coming today; especially Ed who has taken the time and trouble to decorate the shop and to provide free fish and chips as a wedding present for us." Lyn started a round of applause, and Ed bowed in appreciation.

"Secondly, I want to thank my mother-in-law and her brother Jeff for travelling all this way to the wedding." She turned to them and smiled. "And lastly I want to thank Neil for wanting to continue putting up with me for the rest of his life. Neil, as some of you may know, is not good at speeches, and so as I've arranged it all I suppose I have to do the honors." She looked fondly at her husband. "Also, I expect the news has got around that we'll soon be moving back down to Surrey to be near Maggie and family again, and also so that Neil can start to see his son Billy and get to know him. But all is not lost; we'll still be coming back now and again to stay at the cottage in the summer, and we'll be re-painting the café every Spring." She smiled as the guests clapped and cheered. "Anyway, all I've got left to say is enjoy your fish and chips everyone, and afterwards the girls will tune up and play a few songs."

Listening to the foot-stamping appreciation from the guests as she sat down, Lyn realised she had not felt nervous at all and in fact could freely admit to herself with some degree of certainty that their second wedding had been infinitely preferable to the first.

CHAPTER 51

SHE HAD JUST finished the month-end accounts when the phone call came.

"Hi Lyn!"

"Hey Sara! Are you okay? Everything alright at the café?" She immediately started to worry.

"The café's doing great; in fact much better than last season so far."

"That's good news. How's the new girl shaping up?"

"Fine. Reggie's stayed on after all, and the three of us seem to make a good team. But the café's not why I phoned."

"Oh?"

"I thought I'd tell you the news."

"What's that then?"

"Peter came in for some lunch the other day with a lady. It appears they're going to get married. He's really changed; much more laid back now. He was even wearing shorts and sandals!" She chuckled as she spoke.

"Wow! Who is she?"

"Her name's Nancy, and they met through Friends Reunited. Apparently they knew each other years ago, but it seems they sort of drifted apart. I think after your wedding he probably waited for you to come back, but after a year he obviously accepted that you were staying where you are."

"Poor Peter. I think he's a very lonely man." Lyn sighed and tried not to feel guilty all over again.

"Not any more. She's a very nice lady; a widow, with two grown-up daughters and a son, and five grandchildren. Peter's suddenly got the family he should have had in the first place."

"Tell him I'm so pleased. He deserves to be happy. He's a good man." Lyn suddenly felt as if a great weight had been taken off her shoulders.

"He's told Nancy all about you. She wants you and Neil to come to their wedding. She says without you he would never have felt lonely enough to get back in touch with her."

"Oh, God, no. Neil would never go." She found herself shaking her head as she laughed down the phone line.

"Try and persuade him. It'll be good to see you again, Lyn."

"We're coming up to the cottage when Neil takes a fortnight off at the end of August."

"Shame. The wedding's on August 6th."

"Sorry, but do give him my regards."

"Will do."

"Do I want to go to your ex-boyfriend's wedding?" That's a toughie." Neil did not even try to hide the sarcasm.

"How about just to the church then? His fiancée wants to meet me."

"You go if you want to. I'll be washing my hair that day."

"You haven't got any hair."

"I'll be slashing my wrists then."

"Come on; if you take a fortnight off at the beginning of August instead we can go to the wedding, check things are okay at the café, and then spend the rest of the time lazing on the beach. It'll be getting colder again in September."

"Oh, for fuck's sake!" He rolled his eyes and bashed his forehead on a nearby wall.

"Thanks darling. I take it that's a 'yes' then?

They stood apart from the family in the churchyard under a yew tree, glad of its shade from the searing heat. She tried to block out the sound of her husband grumbling about wearing a suit and tie in the height of summer, and concentrated on the look of happiness on the faces of the bride and groom.

"Have we got to pose for the photos, or can we go now?" Neil puffed and loosened his cravat.

"No, we'll be in the 'friends' group with Jamie and Sara, Caroline and Reggie."

"Then can we go?"

"Stop being such a miserable old git." She noticed Peter waving them over. "Come on, it's our turn."

"Lyn and Neil! Thanks so much for coming today. It means a lot to us."

She was aware of Neil's silence as Peter kissed her on both cheeks:

"Thank you for asking us. Sara told me about how you and Nancy met." She shuffled into place for the group photo, linking arms with Neil on one side and Jamie on the other.

"It's like a fairytale, Lyn. I hope you and Neil are coming to the evening do?" Nancy looked towards her as the photographer set up his camera.

"You'd better, or I'll make you sit on the bike for the whole two hundred miles home." Jamie squeezed her arm and nudged her leg with his own.

"It's laugh-a-minute boy here. He doesn't want to go." She whispered in Jamie's ear.

"I'll show him my new Harley; well, it's not new as such, but it's a Harley." Jamie whispered back.

"What are you two whispering about?" Neil looked thunderously at her.

"Jamie's got a Harley." She smiled as the camera clicked. "Yeah?"

"Apparently. Is that good?" She turned to face him. "All look this way please!" The photographer held up his hand.

"Bloody hell, yeah." A smile played around Neil's lips.

"Perfect!" The photographer clicked away.

"He'll bring it tonight to the evening do."

"Bastard."

It was one of the more upmarket hotels in St. Ives. The function room was exquisitely decorated to match the bride's peach and cream outfit. As she waltzed with Peter around the dance floor, Lyn noticed how much more relaxed he seemed.

"She's good for you, Peter." Lyn followed his lead. "I never realised what a great dancer you are."

"It's all Nancy's doing. We have ballroom dancing lessons once a week, and meet up with her friends at tea dances on Saturday afternoons. It's all very civilized." He twirled her around once, and then once more for good measure.

"Do you get on well with her family?"

"Her husband died quite young, and the children have taken to me as a second father. I've never been surrounded with so many people before. Come and say hello to her."

As she walked up to the top table with him he turned towards her.

"Where's Neil?"

"Outside looking at Jamie's Harley. It was the only way I could get him here tonight."

"I'd like to shake his hand and say no hard feelings." "If you can get him away from the bike.

"Hello Lyn." Nancy stood up and walked around to kiss her.

"Nancy, it was a beautiful wedding, and you look absolutely stunning." Lyn gave the older woman a hug.

"Peter's told me so much about you. I've got you to thank for us meeting up again after all these years."

"I wasn't the right one for him, but thank goodness he found somebody who was! I can see the change in him already."

"Your husband seems a little edgy." Nancy chuckled and indicated with a nod of her head towards the back of the room.

Lyn turned around to see Jamie coming towards them, whilst Neil stood and glowered by the door. Peter took his cue and walked back towards Neil.

"He's getting a bike now, Lyn!" Jamie shouted. "And it's all my fault!"

"Oh, God. Now it'll be bits of engine on my kitchen table and a house stinking like a tannery."

She looked towards Neil and Peter at the back of the room. Peter had extended his arm to Neil, who to her surprise was smiling as he shook the proffered hand.

She turned back to Jamie, who had also witnessed the scene.

"Thank goodness for that. I was dreading those two meeting up."

Jamie waved away her fears:

"Before you know it, he'll be giving Peter a lift on the back of his bike."

CHAPTER 52

HIS FINE DARK hair had a slight russet hue, the colour of leaves in the autumn. Lyn kissed the top of her stepson's head as she bent down to put a Thomas the Tank Engine birthday cake in front of him that she had been preparing for most of the week before.

"Billy, look! You're having another birthday party today with Daddy, Lyn, Granny and Uncle Jeff! Who's a lucky boy then?"

Three-year-old Billy smiled and looked appreciatively at his cake:

"I lucky. Where's my Mummy?" He looked around the kitchen and then back to his cake.

"Mummy will see you later on when Daddy takes you home." Lyn felt a momentary stab of jealousy, but then shrugged it off and thanked her lucky stars that they had been granted access every other weekend.

"Okay. I want cake."

"What's the magic word, Billy?" Neil took hold of his son's fingers and smiled at him.

"Peeeaas!"

"That's good enough. But first, you have to blow out your candles and make a wish."

Lyn watched as her husband struck a match and Billy reached out a hand:

"The candles are hot, Billy. You can blow them out, but don't touch them." She gently lowered his fingers. "Are we all ready to sing 'Happy Birthday'? Ready with the camera, Maggie?"

"Of course. I want a new picture for my wall."

Her eyes filled with tears as the little boy sang along with them almost word for word in perfect pitch, and then blew out the candles with one big puff.

"Did you make a wish?"

"Yes." The child nodded his head furiously.

"What did you wish for?" She cut a piece of cake and put it in front of him.

"That Daddy, you, Mummy, Rob and me all live in one big house!" He held his arms up wide.

"That would be nice, but Mummy and Rob have their house and Daddy and I have this one."

"Let's move on from that one, eh?" Neil cut himself a slice of cake and sat down at the table.

"He's just a little boy. He sees things in black and white." Lyn smiled at Billy, who grinned back at her with a mouth full of cake crumbs. "It's nearly time to open your present! Are you ready?"

"Where's my present?" Billy nodded as he finished his cake.

"It's just outside. Let me wipe your hands and then you can go and see it." Lyn cleaned up the cake residue as best she could and then followed the others into the garden, where a large gift-wrapped object stood on the patio.

"Can I open it?" Billy's eyes were like saucers.

"Sure can. Do you need any help?" Neil squatted down so that he was on a level with his son.

"No. I do it my own."

"Okay. You open it yourself then." Neil chuckled at the turn of phrase, and turned his camera on.

"Wow!" Billy tore at the rest of the paper to uncover a shiny red pedal car in the shape of a Ferrari.

"Do you like it?"

Neil's question went unanswered as Billy sat in the car and disappeared noisily up the garden path.

"One satisfied customer." Jeff sat down in a deckchair and grinned.

"Oh to be three again. I'm going to punch the next person that comments on how much my 'grandson' looks like me." Neil sank down in a deckchair next to Jeff and sighed.

"Let people think what they like, son. They will anyway. What does that make me - bloody Methuselah's missus?" Maggie rested her head back on a bench and closed her eyes. "I'm not far off ninety years of age now. It's scary as hell." She trailed off and began to doze in the sunshine.

"How can my mother be ninety?" Neil kept his eyes on Billy. "Time needs to stand still for a little while so I can watch my little son grow up."

"If time's standing still he won't be growing." Jeff answered laconically from the depths of his deckchair before falling asleep.

Lyn smiled at the sight of the two old people napping.

"Neil; we've got plenty of years left yet. Don't worry about getting old."   Lyn waved to Billy at the end of the garden, who waved back.

"It would just be nice to have my time all over again so that I could put right all the mistakes I've made."

"Such as?"

"Causing my wife so much pain and sorrow that she left me."

Lyn pulled a chair over to where her husband was sitting and planted a kiss on the top of his head before sitting down.

"We'd never have got Billy if you hadn't. There's a silver lining to every cloud. Look on the bright side. You have a beautiful son."

"You're right, doll, but it doesn't excuse my behavior."

"I've got my menopause, and you've had your man-o-pause; that makes us about even, I'd say." She laughed and covered one of his hands with her own. "But isn't it strange how a man's menopause entails having affairs and buying motorbikes, while a woman has to put up with dry nethers, aching joints, and hot flushes. Perhaps I should try the affair bit? If Peter ever gets divorced and you've had enough of me, maybe I'll give him another go." She winked at him.

"No chuffing way. I'm here to stay."

He kissed her and ruffled her hair. She watched fondly as Neil stood up to meet his son, who pedaled his racing car furiously back down the path.

"Daddy; what's that?" He pointed to a large covered object standing by the side of the house.

"That's Daddy's motorbike.   Would you like to sit on it?"

"Yes." Billy nodded.

Neil lifted up the boy and carried him over to the bike.

"That's a Honda Fireblade. After you and Lyn it's the best thing that a man can have. When you ride it and see the open road in front of you and feel the wind in your face, you're gone in your head to somewhere far away. One day I'll teach you to ride it if I'm not too old." He took off the cover and lowered his son down gently down onto the seat.

"Wow!"

Billy made appreciative noises as Lyn picked up her camera:

"You'll never be too old, Neil. Sit behind him on the seat and I'll take a picture of the pair of you."

"I'll be in my seventies before he's riding bikes." Neil sat down and sighed as he held the boy closer.

"I'm sure the pair of you will have the time of your lives!"

With Billy safe between his father's arms she snapped away before the moment was lost forever.

THE END

If you have enjoyed this story, you may also wish to check out 'The Pilates Class', another humorous book by Stevie Turner.

REVIEWS OF 'THE PILATES CLASS'
BY STEVIE TURNER

"Once again, Stevie Turner did not disappoint with THE PILATES CLASS. I just love her sideways take on reality. This novel is chock-full of humorous characters that will have you laughing the moment you crack the book. With the aim of rehabilitating his injured shoulder, Roger Harvey's doctor prescribes several free sessions in a Pilates class, and this where the fun begins. You will totally relate to the varied and idiosyncratic personalities of the class members. This read is definitely worth your while." - *Cynthia B Bergstrom*

"Have to say, that when I began reading, I anticipated something much lighter, more flip and shorter in duration. BIG, pleasant surprise! This is a slice of real life, played out by characters we might have in our families or neighborhoods. Using the Pilates class as the stage, creates a common denominator that brings everyone to a level playing field. The love/hate relationships keeps this believable as well as entertaining. Entertaining enough to help you through those moments when reality rears its less than desirable head. We create our own happiness in life, and this book is a celebration of that truth." – *Annette Rochelle Aben*

OTHER BOOKS BY STEVIE TURNER

THE PILATES CLASS
A HOUSE WITHOUT WINDOWS
FOR THE SAKE OF A CHILD
LILY: A SHORT STORY
NO SEX PLEASE, I'M MENOPAUSAL!
A RATHER UNUSUAL ROMANCE
THE DAUGHTER-IN-LAW SYNDROME
REVENGE
THE NOISE EFFECT: A SHORT STORY
THE DONOR
LIFE: 18 SHORT STORIES
WAITING IN THE
WINGS MIND GAMES
REPENT AT LEISURE
A NOVELLA COLLECTION
CRUISING DANGER
ALYS IN HUNGERLAND

www.ingramcontent.com/pod-product-compliance
Lightning Source LLC
Chambersburg PA
CBHW061229210726
48293CB00003B/707